LOVE & RIVALRY

LOVE &
RIVALRY

*Three Exceptional
Pairs of Sisters*

BY DORIS FABER

ILLUSTRATED WITH PHOTOGRAPHS

The Viking Press
New York

For my sister

First Edition · Copyright © 1983 by Doris Faber: All rights reserved
First published in 1983 by The Viking Press, 40 West 23rd Street, New York, New York 10010
Published simultaneously in Canada by Penguin Books Canada Limited
Printed in U.S.A.   1   2   3   4   5   87   86   85   84   83

Library of Congress Cataloging in Publication Data
Faber, Doris, 1924–Love and rivalry.
Bibliography : p.   Includes index.
1. Sisters—United States—Biography—Juvenile literature.   2. Stowe, Harriet Beecher, 1811–1896—
Juvenile literature.   3. Cushman, Charlotte, 1816–1876—Juvenile literature.   4. Dickinson, Emily,
1830–1886—Juvenile literature.   5. Novelists, American—19th century—Biography—Juvenile
literature.   6. Poets, American—19th century—Biography—Juvenile literature.   7. Actresses—
United States—Biography—Juvenile literature.   I. Title.
HQ777.F32 1983   306.8'754'0922   83-6566   ISBN 0-670-44221-6

Page 196 constitutes an extension of the copyright page.

CONTENTS

Contents

vi

Preface

Are big sisters always bossy? Do little sisters always feel a lot of envy? Someday, possibly, someone will put the personalities of millions of sisters into a computer—and come out with somewhat scientific answers to such questions.

But this is a book about people, not statistics. During a good many years of reading and writing biographies, I have been struck by how often sisters have had a significant influence on each other's lives, even long after childhood. Thus I have picked out three pairs of exceptional sisters from the American past who exemplify the importance of the sisterly relationship.

Right here I want to stress that everything in the following pages is solidly based on fact. Whenever anybody speaks, the words have been taken directly out of old letters or diaries or memoirs; more details regarding my sources will be found in the Notes and Bibliography.

I should point out, also, that we shall be looking into lives illuminating a previously neglected facet of the female experience—in effect, delving into a new area of women's history. But girls from well-off or at least well-established families were far more likely to leave a written record than girls from less privileged backgrounds. That is why the three sets of sisters I have chosen had quite similar heredity; they were all New Englanders, white, and Protestant. Nevertheless, men from the same limited stream dominated the public affairs of the young United States, so its women fairly represent the mainstream's feminine component.

Most importantly, though, the lives of Catharine and Harriet Beecher, of Charlotte and Susan Cushman, of Emily and Lavinia Dickinson are interesting. Of course, the achievements that have made at least some of these names famous heighten our curiosity, and yet the personal lives of all six contain such a variety of emotional episodes that they might be described, just a little flippantly, as pure soap opera. Upon these personal lives, especially their sisterly love and rivalry, we shall now focus.   D. F.

· I ·

Catharine Beecher
and
Harriet Beecher Stowe

The Connection Is Settled

To start with, we must forget ever having heard the name Harriet Beecher Stowe. Of course, back in the 1850s she wrote *Uncle Tom's Cabin*, which helped to cause the Civil War, besides making her one of the most famous women in American history. Right now, though, it is plain Hattie Beecher whom we have to imagine, growing up in the pretty Connecticut village of Litchfield, constantly harried and diverted by her big sister Katy.

Altogether, Hattie had seven brothers and three sisters. Five babies had preceded her, and five more would follow her, so she came exactly in the middle among the offspring of the Reverend Lyman Beecher. Katy, quite differently, was the eldest of the lot. Since these two present such an outstanding example of the way sisterly emotional ties can continue exerting a powerful influence far beyond childhood,

2

and also to avoid confusion, we shall pay scant attention to many of their relatives. Nevertheless, we must first of all meet their father.

A man who climbed fruit trees faster than any of his boys, the Reverend Beecher ruled his brood exuberantly—"No crying!" he would shout. "Look pleasant!" With lovable quirks galore, he deserves his reputation as a real old New England character. The passage of time, however, has made him seem somewhat less lovable, inasmuch as he was a fierce upholder of the rigid Puritan faith of his forebears that has long since lost its appeal. In addition, he valued boys immeasurably more than girls because they could grow up to be ministers.

Concerning his first wife—Katy and Hattie's mother—less can be said because Roxana Foote Beecher did not live long enough to have much effect on either of her memorable daughters. Yet she had unusual intelligence and a saintly disposition, without much outward beauty, all of which undoubtedly contributed toward the problems of the girls she produced.

Katy and Hattie were not close in age; ten years plus three months separated them. This at least partly explains why Katy bossed Hattie to such an extent, and why Hattie uncomplainingly accepted the bossiness. For instance, during the winter in which Hattie was going on eleven, she was sent to visit her grandmother and an unmarried aunt, where Katy wrote to her:

> I suppose you will be very glad to hear you have a little sister at home. We have no name for her yet.
>
> We all want you home very much, but hope you are now where you will learn to stand and sit straight, and hear what people say to you, and sit still in your chair, and learn to sew and knit well, and be a good girl in every particular; and if you don't learn while you are with Aunt Harriet, I am afraid you never will.

For the sake of fairness—and big sisters need not fear that they will always be seen at their worst in these pages—the next several sentences of Katy's letter should also be considered. In these she warmly assured

Hattie that Old Puss, the senior of the family's troop of cats, sent his respects. With its loving mixture of sermonizing and high spirits, the letter might have been dashed off by the Reverend Beecher himself.

Indeed, Catharine Esther Beecher at the age of twenty-one amazingly took after their father. As his firstborn, she was without question his favorite—"Oh, thou little immortal!" he had cried when she had been placed in his arms in the opening year of the century, on September 6, 1800. Her arrival in the first year of his first pastorate struck him as a great good omen.

Thus he had with his own hands constructed a small wooden seat in which she could ride beside him as he drove his buggy around that first parish of East Hampton at the far end of Long Island. Isolated from New York City by miles of sand, but an easy sail from his native Connecticut, the area then had a distinctly New England flavor. Here he had taught Catharine to fish just as if she were a boy, and he had tested her in ways that might horrify other parents. Once he had swung her by her wrists out of the garret window to see if she would be frightened: she was not frightened a bit.

Though he soon had several cherished sons, Catharine's father never lost his special tenderness toward her. Even so, and no matter that she proved to have an exceptionally keen mind, his own mind was too set in the old Puritan mold to think of any future for her except a suitable marriage. As early as 1810, a few months before Katy's tenth birthday, while the family was traveling to its new home in Litchfield and their wagon rumbled past Yale College, the Reverend Beecher had simply ignored her as he gestured excitedly. "There, boys, look there!" he hollered to her younger brothers. "There's where you've got to go one of these days."

Certainly nobody alive then was likely to dream that any female would ever attend Yale. The world of Catharine's girlhood judged that fine embroidery ought to occupy any young lady until she found a husband, and into this same world Harriet Elizabeth Beecher was born the following year, on June 14, 1811. It is worth remembering that babies no longer were a novelty in her family by then. Being slight and quiet, Hattie might easily have felt neglected, if not for Katy.

For their mother was not just too busy to lavish affection on her latest infant. She had already lost any capacity to feel deeply about either the joys or sorrows of her life on earth. To understand her, it is helpful to know something of her background.

By the measure of those who valued money beyond any spiritual goods, Roxana Foote had been above the lovably uncouth but extremely religious Lyman when he came courting her. He was descended from blacksmiths and farmers—he still said "critter," instead of "creature," even after his years at Yale—while she had a prosperous grandfather who had been personally acquainted with George Washington and then had served in Connecticut's legislature. On old General Ward's gentlemanly estate near the Connecticut shore, Roxana and her sisters spent hours at their spinning wheels, but they also learned French and the elements of natural science.

Still, Lyman's gusto not only captured Roxana's heart, it made her almost selfless. He had warned her that his quick temper could not endure any contradicting, and she somehow managed never to cross him: she became his very model of a saintly wife. Bearing eight babies, serenely coping with all sorts of domestic turmoil, even teaching a day school in the family parlor and squeezing a few boarders into the upstairs bedrooms to help make ends meet, Roxana showed no regrets—but she showed scarcely any other feelings, either.

No wonder, then, that when Hattie's best-loved kitten developed alarming symptoms and had to be put out of its misery, it was Katy to whom Hattie ran for comfort. Katy's effect on the oddly thoughtful Hattie went much deeper, though, than incessant prodding softened by daily little encouragements and sympathy. Through her, Hattie came under the spell of their mother's sister Mary.

Years before Hattie's birth, Aunt Mary had begun giving Katy a warmth that her own mother could not offer. Aunt Mary hugged her for no particular reason; she convinced the child that nobody else had the equivalent skill at finding the freshest egg in the hen house—"She was the poetry of my childhood," Catharine recalled long afterward. Yet the fascinating Aunt Mary had suffered incredibly.

The details of Aunt Mary's terrible experience would have been only whispered in the early 1800s, because children then were not supposed to know anything about sexual relationships, particularly those that occurred outside of a conventional marriage. Still, the young Katy did grasp the gist of the unspeakable truth.

When Aunt Mary had been only seventeen, she had enchanted a Mr. Hubbard, a merchant with extensive property in the West Indies. In sedate Connecticut youthful Mary was dazzled by the prospect of living on a tropical plantation, and she let Mr. Hubbard prevail upon her family to approve an early marriage. Then her arrival at her husband's plantation shocked her almost out of her mind.

For she found children of obviously mixed race in the West Indies household that her marriage vows made her the mistress of, and she found a black slave woman who was their mother. Most sinfully, Mary's new husband blandly admitted that he was these children's father. Mary must not be silly—why not just accept this common practice?

No! Brought up to believe that only death could sever the marriage bond, Mary prayed to die. And her health failed until a physician decreed that the hot climate of the Caribbean was killing her. The verdict made it possible for the young Mrs. Hubbard to sail back alone to New England, where her sister Roxana sought her help in training her own daughters.

Aunt Mary achieved more than she would ever realize. Decades later Harriet Beecher Stowe would testify about her: "What she saw and heard of slavery filled her with constant horror and loathing. She has said that she often sat by her window in the tropical night, when all was still, and wished that the island might sink in the ocean, with all its sin and misery, and that she might sink with it."

But Aunt Mary died when Hattie was just two years old. It was Katy who had heard these words and repeated them. From Katy—in a tidy New England town where nobody kept slaves, and the few colored servants at least had their freedom—the young Hattie absorbed such an intense feeling of slavery's immorality that, as a grown woman, she would be sure it had come from Aunt Mary herself.

No male in the family could have spoken on the subject to a girl— nor could Hattie's mother have conveyed the smoldering emotion that would later inflame Hattie's gifted imagination. Roxana Beecher, harboring latent infection from the lung disease that had killed Mary, collapsed and died of tuberculosis three years later, when Hattie was not yet six. Significantly, Harriet made another mistake in her maturity about her own age at the time of her mother's death.

Priding herself, with reason, on having a wonderfully reliable memory, she still claimed she had been only three when her mother died. It is not hard to explain this error, though, because she really had been deprived of her mother's close attention before her second birthday by a younger brother. And then another baby boy compounded her loss in the same year that her mother's death ended any possibility that she might achieve the happiness of wholehearted maternal love. As a result, she would for the rest of her own life attempt to make up for what she had missed by fervently exalting the ideal of motherhood.

In doing so, she followed Katy's example. Sixteen when their mother died, Katy wrote an ode of many stanzas commemorating the tragic event. Temporarily, their father's unmarried sister moved in to supervise the household, with Katy as her main deputy. Then, within a year, Lyman's acute grief at his loss of Roxana healed to the point that he brought a proper new bride from Boston, coincidentally named Harriet, whom Katy dutifully welcomed.

Harriet Porter Beecher soon was enlarging the family in the rambling white-frame parsonage with two more boys and a girl. Like her predecessor, the second Mrs. Beecher had an aristocratic background appreciated by her husband's unusually elite congregation, which included several retired judges and wealthy lawyers. Also like Roxana, her successor possessed a conscientious, religious nature, combined with a temperament lacking warmth. Since she faced the further handicap of having to meet constant comparison with a saintly legend, she inspired more obedience than love among the eight stepchildren whose care she bravely undertook.

Little Hattie surely tried to win her affection. To her new mother, the six-year-old child humorously promised, "Because you have come and married my pa, when I am big enough I mean to go and marry your pa." Even so, the second Mrs. Beecher's weight of domestic responsibilities prevented the development of much rapport, and Hattie increasingly seemed strangely pensive. Owl-eyed, her father laughingly called her.

Only the most tractable of Roxana's three daughters adjusted to the change easily. For three there were—Sister Mary, five years younger than Katy, almost six years older than Hattie, was eleven at the time of their mother's death. Neither before then nor ever afterward would Sister Mary do anything surprising. But as the overwhelming drama of Katy's life approached, Sister Mary played at least a minor part.

By the age of twenty Katy was full of conflicting feelings. From as far back as she could remember, she had been trying to make the best of her limited feminine beauty, coaxing her silky brown hair into long lustrous curls. But she could not fail to notice her other defects, especially the prominence of her Beecher nose. "Catharine is not handsome," the second Mrs. Beecher confided to Boston, adding diplomatically, "yet there is hardly any one who appears better." In fact, Katy resembled her father outwardly as well as in her personality, which her era could only deplore.

Because she did have so much of his gusto Katy wasted no energy wishing she were the sort of girl that easily attracts beaux. The only male whose approval she craved was her own father, and his regard she had never had to worry about. Still, as the girls with whom she had attended classes at Miss Pierce's began marrying, the Reverend Beecher distressed his eldest daughter more than once by saying that soon it would be Katy's turn.

Then Katy suddenly found herself entertaining a suitor so far out of the ordinary that she felt unutterably confused. At twenty-five,

Alexander Metcalf Fisher was already a professor of mathematics at Yale, with such a prodigious aptitude in several branches of higher learning that many of his colleagues believed he was bound to become America's most eminent scientist. Yet he was also interested in poetry—and he was very lonely. That was how he first happened to visit Litchfield one Sunday afternoon.

Katy had often scribbled nonsense verse on such subjects as the plague of rats that afflicted the parsonage attic in spite of the vigilance of the Beecher cats. The Reverend Beecher could only approve, however, when his eldest daughter produced a more serious effort, and he therefore encouraged her to send it to a religious journal that frequently printed his own sermons. In due course the paper published "The Evening Cloud," making it possible for Professor Fisher to read:

> *See yonder cloud along the West*
> *In gay fantastic splendour dress'd . . .*
> *But short its evanescent stay,*
> *Its brilliant masses fade away.*
>
> *Thus to fond man, does Life's fair scene*
> *Delusive spread its cheerful green . . .*
> *But one by one his hopes decay,*
> *Each flattering vision fades away. . . .*

And naught remains, Katy at some length concluded, but heaven. To a solemn young man, the idea of meeting "the poetess of Litchfield" became irresistible, so he journeyed there in the company of a minister already acquainted with the Reverend Beecher. Katy's father instantly grasped Professor Fisher's outstanding possibilities as a son-in-law. Katy, however, could not share her father's enthusiasm.

For Professor Fisher seemed so enormously solemn. Tall, thin, and bespectacled, but, even less promising, as chill in his manner as a February icicle, this young man disturbed Katy mightily. Could she give up such a father as hers in favor of mere position as the wife of a scientific genius? How could it be possible to bear the inevitable burdens of domesticity without the solace of an affectionate husband? Why, in fact, did her father keep alluding to the benefits of the connection when the tongue-tied professor, during repeated visits, spoke only on impersonal topics?

In her quandary Katy behaved as any similarly baffled young woman of her day was expected to. She pretended to a total lack of interest— and went off to teach drawing at a girls' school in New London, Connecticut. Since she had been giving such instruction at Miss Pierce's in Litchfield, she had no difficulty in securing the more distant post, or in finding a respectable New London family where she could board during the term.

But Professor Fisher followed her to New London, and there he discovered an ability to speak passionately. He also offered a plain gold ring that had been his mother's. All Katy's resistance melted then and, happy beyond expression, she wrote home that she was *an engaged woman.* Befitting her new dignity, she signed herself Catharine. As the Reverend Beecher put it complacently in a subsequent letter to relations, "the connection is settled."

Then Catharine arranged to have Sister Mary serve as her substitute while she herself went home to Litchfield, not merely to help their stepmother through a new pregnancy but also to sew her own sheets for her future life in New Haven. Still, there would be ample time for all the stitching because Professor Fisher had already committed himself to another adventure that would keep them apart for at least a year. On behalf of Yale, he was pledged to sail to Europe to investigate the methods and the apparatus used at the universities on the other side of the Atlantic for the teaching of science. It was a splendid opportunity that Catharine could not begrudge him.

So she remained in Litchfield while Professor Fisher sailed from New York on April 1, 1822, aboard the *Albion,* a ship of the latest design.

"I Am Changed..."

TWO months elapsed, and Catharine heard not a word from her dearest friend. She was aware, though, that mail between Europe and America often was delayed, so she felt no great concern. Nowadays, more than a hundred and fifty years later, it is hard for us to realize how patient everybody had to be before inventions like the telegraph, let alone the telephone and television, made good news—and bad—travel swiftly.

Not until the second of June did the Litchfield stagecoach bring a letter for Catharine. Then she knew the worst almost immediately. The handwriting was her father's—he was attending a meeting of ministers in New Haven—and just one glimpse at his opening sentences threw his eldest daughter into a tempest of sobbing.

The Reverend Beecher had written:

> My dear Child,
>   On entering the city last evening, the first intelligence I
> met filled my heart with pain. It is all but certain that Pro-
> fessor Fisher is no more . . .

For the *Albion* had struck rocks off the cost of Ireland during a horrendous windstorm, sinking as it smashed. And only one passenger had managed to swim to shore. The survivor was not Professor Fisher—Catharine's intended husband never would return to her.

Yet her misery throughout the ensuing year went far beyond any personal grief. Suddenly she was forced to agonize over the soul of her loved one and its fate for all eternity. Had she been encouraged to picture him in heaven, she thought she might accept her own loss without too much bitterness, but she was given no such consolation. Instead, she had to visualize him, day and night, enduring the torments of hell.

A century and a half after Catharine's bereavement, it is hard to realize that religion could be as cruel as it was in her day. But the faith of the Reverend Beecher was grim indeed. With his compelling hold on the minds and emotions of his daughters, he caused incalculable suffering for both Catharine and Harriet.

Warmhearted as he was himself, he above all believed in the wrath of God rather than His love. He therefore preached that everlasting damnation must be the lot of most mortals, and he even held that good deeds, during a whole lifetime, could scarcely affect the salvation of any soul. If this seems impossibly harsh, we must remember that the Puritan faith had originally flourished when starvation or savage Indians were real, unceasing threats, so a harsh religion suited those strong enough to survive these earthly perils. Already, by Lyman Beecher's era, there was enough pressure against the strict doctrines he taught to make it clear in Boston, if not Litchfield, that his rigidity was becoming outdated. Poor Catharine! Had she known this, she would have been spared terrible pain.

As it was, she wept morning and evening at her father's severity. To him, only a mysterious experience—a sort of inner vision—could bring any individual into the select company of those chosen for eternal salvation. Though Professor Fisher had earnestly sought this light, he had not found it prior to his departure aboard the *Albion*. Thus Catharine's father, despite his great affection for her, could not comfort her.

"Oh, Edward!" She appealed to her favorite brother, who was studying for the ministry at Yale and had deeply admired Professor Fisher. "Where is he now?"

Edward summoned up more compassion than their father. "Mr. Fisher, I hope and believe, is not lost," he replied.

At least partly owing to Edward's support, Catharine gradually found the strength to challenge the Reverend Beecher himself. In doing so, she revealed an unsuspected ability to develop theories independently and to demolish other ideas that struck her as wrong. What a minister she would have made! But the prevailing attitude toward females in the early nineteenth century kept her from even dreaming of such a career.

Limited not only by other people's convictions about the proper sphere for women, but also by her own desire to avoid antagonizing her father, whom she still idolized, Catharine restricted herself in a manner that future generations cannot easily comprehend. She did not even break away from the church, although she had at least partly discarded its doctrines.

Among the Beecher family she was still regarded with awe. Eleven-year-old Hattie silently shivered at the fearful drama of which Sister Katy was the heroine; the child would never forget any detail of her eldest sister's tragic romance. As for Catharine herself, the experience altered her profoundly.

"I am changed—I am not what I was—I never shall be again," she wrote to a friend from her schooldays. No more a high-spirited girl, she knew that somehow she would have to go on living, but for what purpose? During a visit to Professor Fisher's family in Massachusetts, she stumbled on her answer.

Reading the notebooks that he had filled with his far-ranging inquiries into various branches of knowledge, Catharine concentrated her own mind one day on arithmetic, the next day on astronomy. In her girlhood, she had done well enough at school by merely listening to her instructor and then repeating whatever snippets of information were necessary to obtain praise. Now, as she taught herself geometry, she felt the marvelous elation that comes from engaging in stimulating mental exercise.

This led her to undertake giving lessons in mathematics to Professor Fisher's younger sisters. Then her thrill of accomplishment when she succeeded in communicating her newfound knowledge gave Catharine what she needed—a goal to which she could devote her energy during the rest of her blighted life.

She would do good, she decided, by establishing a school for young ladies where they could acquire a sound grounding in the full spectrum of the sciences, as well as the more usual subjects for female study, such as art and music. And her father raised no objection. Since he considered it unladylike for any female to conduct business dealings, he even rented suitable premises for her school in the Connecticut state capital of Hartford, which at that period lacked an academy for the daughters of its many well-off families. Meanwhile Catharine crammed practically an entire college education into several months of rigorous tutoring by her brother Edward.

Almost precisely a year after the death of Professor Fisher, Catharine opened her school with Sister Mary's assistance. It thrived wonderfully. Soon Miss Catharine Beecher's large classroom in a church basement was providing an exceptional range of educational opportunity to eighty young ladies.

Among the youngest and smallest of the pupils was Sister Hattie. At twelve, indirectly because of Catharine's tragedy, Hattie had turned into quite a trial to her stepmother. Instead of doing as she was bid, she sat, unheeding, her nose buried in a book. For Professor Fisher had willed his own collection of books to Catharine and, following careful study, the Reverend Beecher had decreed that the novels of Sir Walter Scott were not harmful. So Hattie discovered *Ivanhoe*. Thereafter the child became an insatiable bookworm.

Always she had tended to seem removed from whatever was going on around her, with an air of being absorbed in her own thoughts— except that her gray eyes could suddenly show rapt interest. Those eyes were her most noticeable feature; otherwise, she gave an unfortunately mousy impression. Indeed, she would never grow beyond a bare five feet in height.

Yet her mind was acute. At Miss Pierce's school she had already won a prize for her composition on the topic, "Can the Immortality of the Soul Be Proved by the Light of Nature?" Clearly, she, too, was her father's daughter. So it struck him that the best thing for her, young as she was, would be to put her under Catharine's direction in Hartford.

Hattie boarded there with a family whose own daughter, attending Miss Pierce's, was living at the parsonage: that way, no one had to pay any money, and each girl received homelike supervision. Still Hattie felt sure she was getting the better part of the bargain because, for the first time in her life, she had a neat little room all to herself. Here she managed to scribble poetry in secret, while she dreamed of someday writing marvelously romantic tales like Sir Walter Scott's.

Of course, her days were filled with a confusion of lessons and lectures from Catharine. Shy though Hattie was, she even had to serve as an assistant teacher, hearing recitations on religion by girls her own age. Even so, she felt miserable when she was summoned back home after just a few terms of comparative freedom.

But she stayed in Litchfield only briefly, for the Reverend Beecher himself had come to the momentous decision that his message was more urgently needed in the metropolis of Boston. As long ago as his East Hampton days he had nourished wider ambition than a mere country pulpit could satisfy, astounding some of his colleagues by preaching—and printing—fiery sermons on controversial topics. At a meeting of ministers shortly after Aaron Burr killed Alexander Hamilton in a duel, the Reverend Beecher had delivered an unprecedented oration demanding that his fellow clergymen go beyond their religious concerns to condemn all dueling. "Oh, I declare," he liked to reminisce, "if I did not switch 'em and scorch 'em and stamp on 'em. . . . It was the center of old fogyism, but I mowed it down, and carried the vote of the house."

Similarly, he had also started what may have been the first organized campaign against drunkenness with a series of sermons that led to the formation of a temperance society. By such efforts, as well as his outspoken support of traditional Puritanism—for the Reverend Beecher could be either radical or conservative as the spirit moved him—he had made his name known much more widely than his career might suggest. In 1825 he reached the milestone of his fiftieth birthday, and when he was offered the pulpit of a leading Boston church, he leaped at the chance for still wider fame.

It is probable that the second Mrs. Beecher also wished to move. Despite Litchfield's charms, it remained only a village, whereas Boston offered infinitely broader possibilities, including the society of her own relatives. Mrs. Harriet Porter Beecher had, as the years passed, become somewhat less sweet-tempered than in her younger days; even after arriving in Boston, her disposition did not greatly improve. It is probable that the adolescent Hattie bore the brunt of her stepmother's increasing sharpness, for, at fifteen, from Boston, Hattie wrote despairingly to Catharine in Hartford:

> I don't know as I am fit for anything and I have thought that I would wish to die young and let the remembrance of me and my faults perish in the grave rather than live, as I fear I do, a trouble to everyone. Mama often tells me that I am a strange inconsistent being. Sometimes I could not sleep and have groaned and cried till midnight while in the daytime I tried to be cheerful and succeeded so well that Papa reproved

me for laughing so much. I was so absent sometimes that I
made strange mistakes and then they all laughed at me, and
I laughed too though I felt as though I should go distracted.
I wrote rules: made out a regular system for dividing my
time: but my feelings vary so much that it is almost impossible for me to be regular.

Catharine acted swiftly on receipt of this letter. She insisted that
Hattie be returned to Hartford and, furthermore, she insured her own
around-the-clock superintendence over her suffering young sister. What
she arranged was nothing less than a new outpost of the Beecher
family, in a rented house near her school.

Here Catharine and Mary took up residence, and soon Hattie joined
them. Since running a school allowed little leisure for domestic duties,
Catharine prevailed on their father's sister to come and supervise the
housekeeping. It was an admirable plan, except that Mary preferred
marrying a rising young lawyer named Perkins with whom she soon
established a home of her own.

But the arrangement suited everybody else. It gave Aunt Esther a
most satisfying sense of being needed. It provided Catharine with
comfortable surroundings in which she could carry out her larger plans
with more ease; she was becoming an impressive personage. For young
Hattie the sudden liberation from her stepmother—and her father—
had incalculable benefit.

At this point, Hattie was experiencing her own intense religious
struggle. Back in Litchfield, probably owing to the atmosphere of
crisis attending the death of Professor Fisher, the twelve-year-old
child, walking home alone from church one Sunday noon, had experienced a mystic communion that made her run to her father and
tell him she believed she had found Jesus. Could this be true? The
Reverend Beecher kissed her forehead and welcomed her into the elect.
To strive for the salvation of his beloved children was his highest aim
in life, and he knelt to pray with Harriet on such a joyous occasion.

But second thoughts quickly arose to trouble this religiously zealous father. Hattie was extremely young to have found spiritual peace, though certainly she had showed a notable receptivity, having already memorized dozens of hymns along with great chunks of the Bible. Still, was she sufficiently mature to understand sin? Could she comprehend the meaning of submitting herself wholly to God's will? In the months and years that followed, the Reverend Beecher mercilessly quizzed the child until she lost her bearings and descended into black depression over her failure to meet her dear father's expectations. It was this, even more than her stepmother's nagging, that lay beneath her letter to Catharine.

In Hartford Hattie slowly emerged from her religious floundering. Perhaps as significantly, she also made a friend—the first she had ever had. Georgiana May was a few years older, gentle and thoughtful; to Georgie, Hattie confided her innermost secrets. Someday, Hattie promised Georgie with amazing certainty, someday, beside the sparkling little river where they were now walking, she would, with the riches she earned from writing wonderful stories, build an enormous castle of her own. Just wait and see!

More importantly, in Hartford the dreamy Hattie was forced into real life by her overbearing but caring Sister Katy. Having suppressed her own girlish impulses, Catharine pounced down on Hattie as the child was filling a notebook with a poetic drama laid in the court of the Emperor Nero, and ordered her not to waste time on scribbling elaborate verse. Instead, she thrust forward a book on logic for Hattie to study so that Hattie could teach the subject next term. Yet Catharine had not completely lost her warm and playful streak, and she was always grabbing Hattie's letters home to add a funny postscript. Practically never could Hattie descend into a blue mood without Catharine's rushing to cheer her up.

Nor was Hattie's health neglected. Morning after morning the sisters took lively horseback rides before breakfast. Besides Catharine's new belief in exercise as a daily essential, she also had the idea that learning to mix easily with other people should be included in any educational program. As the hostess at a weekly reception where her students met Hartford's best society, Catharine forbade her young sister to sit quietly in a corner. Drawn out of herself, Hattie exposed a delightful gift for telling humorous stories.

Above all, Catharine in her daily grind of conducting her school required mental agility of Hattie. With Sister Mary now married and no longer available, another teacher, named Mary Dutton, had been recruited to take her place. Still, the school kept expanding, and Catharine had awesome plans for making it the foremost institution devoted to female education in the entire country, so Hattie was pressed into duty to give instruction one day in geography, the next day in botany. Somehow she managed to learn what she had to, then keep order when confronted by dozens of girls, many of them older and more assured than she herself was.

Yet there was an excitement at the school that could not help but be invigorating. Just staying in Catharine's shadow during these years gave Hattie a feeling that nothing was impossible. When even the large church basement proved too confining, the tireless Miss Beecher set an awesome new goal. Now she wanted an entire building— constructed to her own detailed specifications, with ten separate rooms, including a library and an assembly hall—as the future home of the institution she grandly began calling the Hartford Female Seminary.

In February 1827 Catharine began a special series of tea parties for the most prominent wives of Hartford. She was motivated by more than hospitality. Though married women, by law, had no control over their family's wealth, possibly they could persuade their husbands to provide the necessary sponsorship and funds.

Catharine's method of raising money was shrewd, and she explained her project very stirringly. Still, her success in swiftly securing the five thousand dollars her building would cost owed something to the general climate of opinion that was increasingly in favor of improved schooling for girls. During this same period many communities were beginning to offer some form of training beyond just the three R's to their daughters as well as to their sons, and even though most of these efforts were much less ambitious than Catharine's, she was not alone.

Already Emma Willard in New York and Mary Lyon in Massachusetts were advancing similar institutions.

To the people of Hartford, however, the idea of establishing a full-scale female seminary seemed tremendously progressive. Even among the most exalted of its old families, Catharine now was no longer just the Reverend Beecher's eldest daughter—she had become "the brilliant Miss Beecher." So there was a great turnout at the beginning of September 1827 for the dedication of the imposing temple of learning that she had marvelously created to enhance the city, both architecturally and educationally.

The ceremony was held in the shelter of the Grecian-style pillars adorning the front entry, with one of Hartford's leading citizens delivering the formal address marking the occasion. "Woman cannot plead at the bar, or preach in the pulpit, or thunder in the senate house," the speaker reminded the gathering. "Yet hers is no trifling eloquence. Its power . . . is mighty in result." Thus intoned Thomas Gallaudet, the city's noted pioneer in the education of the deaf, while the brilliant Miss Beecher sat decorously silent among the other dignitaries. No matter that she was responsible for the new building, that it was her power Mr. Gallaudet obviously alluded to; it still was not considered fitting for a female to speak at a public event.

Within the limits enforced by law or custom, Catharine nevertheless kept increasing her influence. Since writing was deemed a permissible activity for women, she wrote thoughtful articles on female education that appeared in journals read around the country; soon visitors desiring to see her exceptional school for themselves began arriving from as far away as South Carolina. She also wrote textbooks on moral philosophy and arithmetic.

All this, on top of continuous efforts to raise more money for the support of the new building and for the additional teachers its enrollment of two hundred students required, added to the daily pressures of conducting such a thriving institution—all this inevitably had an effect on Catharine's health and frame of mind. Never very calm, she turned irritably short-tempered. Despite the daily horseback riding, she grew pale. Then the morning came when she simply could not summon sufficient energy to get out of bed.

It was a total collapse, and she seemed almost to welcome it. But if Hattie failed to sympathize as much as Catharine wished her to, Hattie had a good reason. Nobody could have grown up in the same household with the Reverend Beecher without becoming familiar with an ailment jocularly referred to among the family as "the hypo"—short for hypochondria. Throughout his career, whenever his latest enthusiasm was thwarted, the father of these sisters had reacted with sudden, excruciating symptoms. Was it heart disease this time? Or a lung complaint? No matter, he groaned and pleaded that he was dying. Once more Catharine proved to take after him in her extreme reaction to frustration.

Yet it was the Reverend Beecher who magically cured her. Up in Boston, at the beginning of the 1830s, he, too, had suffered a terrible bout of "the hypo," owing to the inability of that great city to appreciate his efforts to preserve it from softheaded Unitarianism. Providentially, however, a call had reached him from the distant settlement of Cincinnati, Ohio. So, instead, he would save the West!

First, though, he thought it only prudent to journey there for a personal investigation of what life might be like a thousand miles away. To go alone did not appeal to him; to accompany him did not appeal to the second Mrs. Beecher. At just the moment when his favorite daughter Catharine felt too weak to lift a pencil, there arrived a letter from him asking if she would consider joining him on a scouting trip across the mountains.

Catharine, again, demonstrated her extraordinary resemblance to him. Of course she could not miss such an opportunity! So she deputized Mary Dutton as acting directress of the Hartford Female Seminary, with Hattie as her first assistant. Surely the two of them could carry on during her absence.

Then Catharine hurried to Boston. From there she and her father departed for Cincinnati at the beginning of the spring of 1832.

Saving the West

"I never saw a place so capable of being rendered a paradise," Catharine wrote glowingly to Hattie from Cincinnati. The Reverend Beecher agreed: he had quickly decided to accept the post he had been offered as the head of the new Lane Theological Seminary. After collecting his family back East, he would return that autumn to crown his career spectacularly—by directing the training of candidates for the ministry, thus preserving the West from unsound religious doctrine.

A similar mission excited Catharine. She had become acquainted with some of the ladies of Cincinnati's leading families, she informed Hattie, and:

> The folks are very anxious to have a school on our plan set on foot here. We can have fine rooms in the city college

building, which is now unoccupied, and everybody is ready to lend a helping hand.

As a result, Hattie soon found herself helping Catharine solve the myriad problems involved in turning over the Hartford school to a nephew of Litchfield's Miss Pierce. Then Hattie—at the age of twenty-one—submitted to being uprooted from the familiar landscape of Connecticut to join a caravan of Beechers en route to a new life in Cincinnati. Even if she had hated the idea, she could not have resisted Catharine's imperious planning on her behalf, but she saw no cause for protest.

Considering herself too homely ever to draw the eye of any possible husband—and too shy to say a word if an eligible male should some-how address her—Hattie was already resigned to becoming an old maid. What matter, then, where she passed her dreary round of days? Still, she also had bright spells when everything around her formed into such droll pictures that she kept the whole family chuckling. At the start of the long trek westward she was in one of her happy moods, as she wrote back to New England:

> Here we are—Noah and his wife and his daughters . . . all dropped down in the front parlor of this tavern about thirty miles from Philadelphia. If today is a fair specimen of our journey, it will be very pleasant, obliging driver, good roads, good spirits, good dinner, fine scenery, and now and then some "psalms and hymns and spiritual songs"; for with George [one of her brothers] on board you may be sure of music of some kind. Moreover, George has provided himself with a quantity of tracts, and he and the children have kept up a regular discharge at all the wayfaring people we encounter. I tell him he is *peppering* the land with moral influence.

Yet the Cincinnati of 1832 proved somewhat less of a paradise than the Reverend Beecher and his eldest daughter had painted it. Founded in the wilderness only a few decades earlier, it retained plenty of reminders of its rough frontier past; pigs still roamed its streets, and its riverfront had not lost its brawling squalor, despite row on row of newer, finer buildings uptown. Here a good many other transplanted New Englanders were creating such a civilized setting that they bragged of living in "the London of the West." Even so, the second Mrs. Beecher mourned her loss of Boston, unconsoled by the handsome house the Lane Seminary constructed for her family.

Hattie, with the flexibility of youth, was less critical, especially because Catharine assigned her a congenial task while she herself was arranging for the opening of her new school. Like the rest of the family, Catharine had been greatly diverted by Hattie's letters during the period of their upheaval. Obviously, this young woman had a talent for sprightly writing—and why not make her use it to some advantage?

So Catharine urged her to compose a new text for the teaching of geography. Hattie plunged into the job with astonishing zeal, producing something unique in schoolbooks then—a story from which students might painlessly learn the length of rivers and the principal exports of foreign countries. The publisher to whom Catharine took the manuscript thought it might have a profitable sale, even to schools in the East. He therefore paid Catharine the respectable sum of three hundred and seventy-five dollars for Hattie's work, which Catharine divided in half, giving Hattie one hundred and eighty-seven dollars and fifty cents.

The money elated Hattie. Till then the notion that she might actually be paid for putting words onto paper had been merely one of her daydreams. But she was much less delighted, a month later, when the local newspapers printed the following advertisement:

A NEW GEOGRAPHY
FOR CHILDREN

Corey & Fairbank have in the press,
and will publish in a few days, a

Geography for Children
with numerous maps and engravings,
upon an improved plan.

By Catharine E. Beecher.

The publisher had, alas, turned Hattie into a literary ghost. Even in Cincinnati the eldest Miss Beecher had already acquired a certain eminence, and the output of her pen would be far more likely to attract notice than a volume attributed to her unknown sister. Yet Hattie seemed crushed by the slight, so the good-hearted Catharine briskly let Corey & Fairbank know that the error must be corrected. Since the book sold steadily, requiring several later printings, subsequent editions recorded a compromise. Though the text had been entirely Hattie's, its title page bore the line: "By C. and H. Beecher."

Despite this indignity, the experience of seeing her own writing in print was one of the highlights of Hattie's first years in Cincinnati. Another was making a new friend—the sweet young wife of her father's main assistant at the Lane Seminary. Hattie wrote to Georgiana May in Hartford: "Let me introduce you to Mrs. Stowe." She was, Hattie said, "a delicate, pretty little woman, with hazel eyes, auburn hair, fair complexion, fine color . . . and a most interesting simplicity and timidity of manner." In short, she combined the pleasing appearance that Hattie wished for, herself, with a meekness that made Hattie feel thoroughly at ease in her presence. Soon Hattie Beecher and Eliza Stowe were spending every spare moment together.

When Catharine's school finally opened, after a variety of vexing delays, Hattie had scant leisure, but whatever time that she did manage to spend with Eliza became more precious than ever. Right from the start the Western Female Institute, as Catharine named the new establishment, seemed plagued by difficulties. Promises of the necessary furniture were not kept, pledges of money to provide other essential improvements failed to be paid. Predictably, all this

25

irritated Catharine. Yet Hattie could scarcely avoid wondering whether the root of the troubles might not lie in her sister's own attitude.

No sooner had Catharine returned to the city as a resident than she began rubbing it the wrong way. Did her new friends think that she, personally, would be engaging in the daily drudgery of teaching? Oh, no! Her health was too uncertain to allow any such exertion. Besides, she could contribute so much more by merely supervising the enterprise while she also conducted an extensive correspondence to keep in touch with the really important people back East. In the recently settled West this air of being above the common herd was not admired.

Catharine's first step toward the elevated status she envisioned for herself was to prevail upon Mary Dutton, in Hartford, to come out and teach at the new Institute. Of course, Hattie would loyally assist the quiet, efficient Miss Dutton, Catharine assumed. Hattie, being incapable of standing up to her sister, could only assent, though her own experience of facing endless recitations day after day made the resumption of this routine most unappealing.

Still, Hattie did need prodding to do anything beyond reading the latest novel she could find. So Catharine's forceful pushes were not entirely unwelcome. Among the cultural advantages bolstering Cincinnati's claim to being the western outpost of America's civilization was a literary society; its Monday evening meetings were attended by the city's most cultivated men and women. Catharine, of course, felt quite at home in this milieu, while Hattie shrank at the presumption of joining a group with such prestige. Catharine not only dragged Hattie to the meetings, she even made her submit a story when a contest was announced.

It was just a character sketch, actually, that Hattie sat down and wrote about their Great Uncle Lot who had raised their father, but she gave such a vivid picture of a crusty old New Englander she had never even seen that she won the first prize of fifty dollars. Furthermore, her piece appeared in the *Western Monthly Magazine,* signed by her own full name of Harriet E. Beecher.

During this period Hattie exposed her innermost self in a letter to

Georgiana May that helps explain why her prize had no great impact on her. Having just read a popular French novel—Mme de Staël's *Corinne,* about a highly emotional woman who had some adventures that might be expected to make a minister's daughter blush—Hattie told Georgie:

> I have felt an intense sympathy with many parts of that book, with many parts of her character. But in America feelings vehement and absorbing like hers become still more deep, morbid and impassioned by the constant habits of self-government which the rigid forms of our society demand. They are repressed, and they burn inward till they burn the very soul, leaving only dust and ashes. It seems to me the intensity with which my mind has thought and felt on every subject presented to it has had this effect. . . . Half of my time I am glad to remain in a listless vacancy, to busy myself with trifles, since thought is pain, and emotion is pain.

So Hattie—outwardly docile, though she might be burning inside—kept right on teaching. And Catharine generously kept on encouraging her to write humorously moralistic little stories. But if Catharine could not be faulted for lacking generosity, she almost totally lacked another quality that could have made a huge difference in her own Cincinnati career.

Tact was what she did not have. Somehow she could not see that behaving like a superior being from "back East" would never endear her in the West. Yet, as her school began losing pupils, she felt a sore need for appreciation and affection.

Catharine herself was only partly to blame for the deterioration in her relationship with her stepmother. The second Mrs. Beecher had never ceased bewailing her departure from Boston, and lately she had sunk into querulous invalidism. The point had been reached when friction between Catharine and her father's wife made her no longer comfortable even just visiting her father's house.

If the idea that perhaps she might still acquire her own home by getting married ever occurred to Catharine, she rejected it. Now she was in her thirties, well beyond the usual age of matrimony; yet it was not uncommon for men who had lost their wives to approach a woman of her years as a second partner. Once in Hartford she had been briefly tempted by such an offer. But she still wore Professor Fisher's plain gold ring in token of her undying devotion to him. Moreover, her exceptional success on her own in Hartford had given her an invincible preference for personal independence, despite the many disadvantages of the unmarried state.

These disadvantages hampering the spinster of Catharine's day can hardly be imagined—they affected every aspect of her life. Only an Aunt Esther, selflessly serving in the household of relatives, stayed within society's restrictions. But Catharine could not, would not, emulate Aunt Esther.

Still, even though she often was tactlessly abrasive, Catharine did have exceptional common sense. She also had exceptional drive and gusto. In a man, her abrasiveness might have been excused and her drive admired. Since she was an unmarried woman, she was considered impossibly domineering.

Inevitably, her school in Cincinnati failed. Then Catharine suffered another collapse, triggered this time by an unfortunate accident when her buggy overturned, injuring one of her legs. Even more the victim of injured pride, she fired off a fierce letter to the newspapers accusing Cincinnati of gross ingratitude, before departing to recoup her health and spirits back in New England.

During those last unhappy weeks Catharine also came as close to quarreling with Hattie as Hattie's timidity allowed. The financial affairs of the defunct school were in a terrible mess, with unpaid bills and no proper records showing where its income from tuition payments had been spent. Catharine's handling of money would always be haphazard, to put it kindly. Yet, in her overwrought state, she accused Hattie of being responsible and demanded that her sister hand over her own savings to satisfy the creditors. Hattie did so, no doubt feeling little sorrow at Katy's impending departure.

Poor Mrs. Stowe

B Y the time Catharine left, Hattie—amazingly—had other plans
herself. The previous summer Hattie had accompanied some
cousins on the long journey eastward so that she could represent the
family at the college graduation of her own favorite brother, Henry.
While she was away, Cincinnati had endured one of its periodic ep-
idemics of cholera, and the delicate Eliza Stowe had not escaped the
disease. Hattie returned to discover that her cherished friend was dead.

The intensity of the grief that consumed Hattie gave her courage
to try to console Eliza's husband, who was prostrated by his own
sudden loss. Then in the weeks and months that followed Hattie's sad
arrival on the scene of the tragedy, as these two shared their sorrow
over Eliza, gradually a new emotion began to stir in both their hearts.

Professor Calvin Ellis Stowe was about as far from the standard image of a romantic hero as a man can be. Plump and round-faced, with hardly any hair on the top of his head, though he had thickets of side-whiskers that were already turning grizzled, he looked much older than the childish-seeming Hattie. In fact, he was then thirty-two, while she was twenty-three. His appearance, however, scarcely mattered to her because she had not the slightest notion of falling in love with him. Yet she did.

His unassuming kindness and his keen New England sense of humor, so similar to hers, vanquished her defenses before she had begun to realize she was being courted. At ease with him, just as if he were one of her family, Hattie, indeed, could be captivating. No longer mousy, she matched his every Massachusetts story, her eyes gleaming, with a comic Connecticut tale of her own. So he found himself, much sooner than he would have believed, harboring the most tender of feelings again.

In their serious moments they both realized that the connection made a great deal of sense. Professor Stowe, for all his erudite grasp of Biblical history, was helpless when it came to picking out a pair of matching socks from his wardrobe. Hattie, despite her daydreaming, thought she understood how to provide domestic comfort, and she now discovered that she had been suppressing a deep longing for the role of wife and mother.

Furthermore, the Professor was her father's right-hand man in his efforts to make the Lane Seminary an outstanding institution. With her own high sense of moral purpose, Hattie rejoiced at her chance to contribute, if only indirectly, toward the success of such a noble endeavor. And so, despite their lingering distress over poor sweet Eliza, Hattie and her Professor, after the lapse of a suitable interval of slightly more than a year, were married quietly in her family's parlor on January 6, 1836. Six months before her twenty-fifth birthday, with her eldest sister a thousand miles away, it seemed that Hattie finally had escaped Catharine's influence.

That did not happen.

During the next fifteen years Hattie Stowe made only the faintest

impress beyond her immediate family, though her very limited renown might have been augmented if she had not increased that family
so rapidly and to such an extent. For she became pregnant within just
a few weeks and gave birth that autumn—to twins.

Since both were girls, they were named, odd as it may seem, after
both wives of their father: Eliza and Harriet. Less than two years later
the twins were joined by Henry, then Fred, then Georgiana, then
Sam, and eventually Charley. Because the Lane Seminary failed to
attract many students, owing to dissension on various issues, the
Stowe household grew ever poorer in the monetary sense as it gained
the riches of more and more children. As a result, their mother found
herself so weighed down by domestic responsibilities that, in desper-
ation, she tried to earn the pay of a nursemaid. How else than with
her pen?

Now that she had a darling little girl called Hattie, she took to
signing her inquiries to the editors of local publications quite elabo-
rately—as Harriet E. Beecher Stowe. Yet the stories she submitted
while she was plagued by constant interruptions were necessarily short
and, for the most part, not a bit memorable. They appeared in weeklies
that filled their columns with trivial fiction; no amount of such un-
distinguished scribbling would ever build their author a castle.

Meanwhile Catharine was making herself by far the best known of
the Reverend Beecher's offspring during this period when most of his
sons were just entering the ministry. Traveling through Ohio, she
had been shocked to see how poorly many Western communities were
educating their children, both boys and girls. In the East, she knew,
there were thousands of pious young women who had no useful work.
It struck Catharine, therefore, that she must organize a national effort
whereby New England's oversupply of unattached females would
teach the West's deprived children.

To say that she alone managed to accomplish this goal would be
overstating the case. For her low tolerance of frustration and her short
temper kept her various committees from resettling more than a few
hundred teachers. Still, the publicity she had the gift of attracting

certainly must have encouraged a good many other adventurous spinsters to leave their homes on their own, even though their motive may have differed from hers. How could it be otherwise? The typical headline on newspaper articles describing her crusade was: WIVES FOR THE WEST!

But if Catharine's earnest efforts sometimes provoked snickers, her reputation as the brilliant Miss Beecher continued to spread. For it must be noted that she could more easily be admired at a distance or in personal encounters lasting no more than a few weeks. On closer or longer acquaintance she usually did rub people the wrong way. Nevertheless, to finance her crusade and to keep herself at the top of her form, she developed a way of life that remarkably suited her.

Since she had the knack of writing clearly, she produced one book after another that earned a fair amount of money. But because she preferred spending what she made on promoting her cause rather than on establishing a solitary home for herself, she simultaneously became a wanderer, forever crisscrossing the country. That she succeeded literarily while she turned into a perpetual traveler would have marked her as exceptional even if nothing else had.

Yet her writing itself merited the attention it received because, year after year, she came forth with books that bore impressive titles, such as *The Duty of American Women to Their Country*. That duty, as she would never cease repeating, had positive—and negative—aspects, neither of which are apt to endear her to the late twentieth century. For she vigorously exalted housekeeping and teaching as woman's only "proper sphere," at the same time condemning any female failure to accept submissively man's "natural" superiority in every other field of endeavor.

More than a hundred years afterward, it may seem startling that these ideas comprised the basic philosophy of a highly intelligent single woman who prized her own independence and conducted her own life in a way that almost deserves today's label of liberated. But consistency cannot be expected from Catharine. Again taking after her·

father, she held tightly to traditional attitudes, adapting them only unpredictably when doing so fit her own purposes.

Of course, she deplored ignorance and immorality. Far more entertainingly she railed at lumpy gravy and tightly laced corsets. On the importance of daily exercise as a requisite for physical fitness, Catharine provided a rare sanity in an era that confined women under layers of cumbersome garments, forbade "unladylike" athletic games, and then was surprised by the prevalence of female pallor.

Yet this homeless wanderer, always on the move, blithely inviting herself for a week or two into the homes of relatives or former students, derived her greatest success from several books in which she told the wives of America precisely how to organize their households. The popularity of these works was based on more than their contents, however. They owed much, in addition, to Catharine's talent for self-advertising.

Wherever she went, she made appointments with members of school boards and presented them with copies of her *Treatise on Domestic Economy for the Use of Young Ladies*. Would this not make an excellent textbook? As a result, it was adopted for classroom use in many areas—so countless young ladies remembered her name when they entered the real world of domesticity. And they kept buying volume after volume of Miss Beecher's works on other topics.

Despite the range of Catharine's activities, however, she did not cease swooping down on the Stowe household in Cincinnati. Her brother-in-law had mixed feelings about her. But her influence over her sister by no means diminished.

Early in the 1840s, when Harriet had accumulated about a dozen short pieces of some literary merit, it was Catharine who insisted these deserved more than fleeting notice. Returning to New York, Catharine handed a sheaf of manuscripts to one of her own publishers, Harper & Brothers, with the promise to provide a preface herself. Thus there soon appeared a volume entitled *The Mayflower, or Sketches of the Descendants of the Puritans,* with an introduction in which the eminent

Miss Beecher identified this book's author as a sister "trained from childhood" under her care. On the identity of that author, Calvin Stowe himself had taken a stand.

"My dear, you must be a literary woman," the Professor wrote to his wife when she informed him, from Hartford, where she had gone to visit Sister Mary, that her book had been accepted. The proud husband added:

> It is so written in the book of fate. Make all your calculations accordingly. Get a good stock of health and brush up your mind. Drop the E. out of your name. It only incumbers it and interferes with the flow and euphony. Write yourself fully and always Harriet Beecher Stowe. . . .

The Professor, however, was less enthusiastic when Catharine lured Harriet to stay a year in the East, recouping her strength at one of Catharine's favorite resorts. It was Dr. Wesselhoeft's sanitorium in Brattleboro, Vermont, where the sisters conscientiously endured being wrapped as mummies every dawn in cold, wet sheets and took icy shower baths several times daily, besides drinking copiously from the medicinal springs on the property. All this regime comprised the "water cure" the German-born doctor had found to be an ideal treatment for almost anything that ailed descendants of America's Puritans. Though their sense of duty would not allow them the indulgence of a vacation, the unpleasantness of intermittent shivering gave them license to enjoy idly strolling through the picturesque countryside for weeks and months of release from the pressures of their ordinary existence.

In the relaxed atmosphere of Brattleboro, Harriet and Catharine renewed their closeness of Litchfield. As a mature woman, Harriet had come to consider her sister "strange, nervous, visionary and to a certain extent unstable." Now she found it possible to overlook Catharine's bossiness and to appreciate her bravery in surmounting personal tragedy. Whatever resentment may have burned within the young Hattie no longer could bother her; one quality shared by these sisters was their inability to bear a grudge. Of Catharine's most recent book Harriet offered high praise. "It is a stroke well aimed, well struck and must do good," she said. "Well done, Katy!"

So it was probably at Brattleboro, in 1846, that Catharine made a new commitment to Harriet. As they both were well aware, Harriet had been able to escape her domestic burdens this year only because of emergency help from some of Professor Stowe's relatives. Once she returned home, she was bound to be swamped again in dirty laundry, sour milk, and all the emotional turmoil of a house filled with children.

Did Harriet feel drawn to attempt a higher form of literature? Even as Catharine asked the question, anticipating its reply, her own response was ready. When she was needed, Catharine promised, she would drop her own work to come and give Harriet a year of freedom from every interruption—so that Harriet could devote herself wholly to *her* writing.

But Professor Stowe had definite ideas of his own on the desirability of having Catharine spend more than a week or two in his home. These stemmed partly from his long-simmering disapproval of the way his wife's sister had treated her before her marriage. Besides, on a few more recent occasions, Catharine had—to use a favorite phrase of his—bamboozled the Professor himself into doing more than he bargained for in support of her grandiose educational scheme.

Thus when Catharine offered a few years later to come and help the Stowes by starting a small school in their Cincinnati front parlor, the Professor exploded. He informed his wife:

> It is as much your duty to renounce Kate Beecher and all her schoolmarms as it is to renounce the Devil and all his works. Kate has neither conscience nor sense—if you consent to take half a pound, she will throw a ton on your shoulders, and run off and leave you, saying—*it isn't heavy, it isn't heavy at all, you can carry it with perfect ease.* I will have nothing to do with her in the way of business, any more than I would with

the Devil . . . and you ought not to have. She would kill off
a whole regiment like you or me in three days.

Yet the good Professor, as is not uncommon among mild men
confronted by a strong-minded woman, was overreacting. What
Catharine had in mind then was really just the sort of day school her
own mother had kept back in East Hampton, and its meager income
might have made life less harrowing for the Stowes during the late
1840s. As it was, these were hard years during which they endured
poverty along with incessant illness, even the shock of a sudden death.

While Professor Stowe himself was at Brattleboro, striving to recover from the worst attack of "the blues" he had ever suffered, Harriet
stayed home, watching over the children, throughout a steamy Cincinnati summer. Despite her frazzling nerves, she managed to keep
writing cheerful letters to her husband—until cholera again struck the
city. Then, within a few weeks, the dreaded symptoms afflicted her
adored eighteen-month-old Sammy. And she could not save him.

The experience of losing the youngest of her precious babies tortured Harriet for many months. Never would she forget how her
heart seemed actually to be breaking as she had to sort through Sammy's little garments in a bureau drawer. It was a gloomy household
to which Professor Stowe returned, and neither he nor his wife could
shake away their intense depression. Harriet's eyes, so inflamed that
she could hardly see, got even worse. For weeks she could not leave
the bedroom she had draped almost in darkness.

Frantic worry about money accentuated the family's other woes.
Right from the beginning, the Lane Seminary had been torn by con-
troversy that had kept it from ever bearing out the Reverend Beecher's
optimistic predictions. So Professor Stowe's salary, never princely,
was reduced some months to absolute zero. Still, with all his gift for
scholarly inquiry, he could not muster the practical ability to seek out
a better-paying position.

Providentially, Bowdoin College in the Maine town of Brunswick
came to the family's rescue in 1849 by offering him a post on its

faculty; nearly thirty years earlier he had been an outstanding student there. Even so, it was not easy for either of the Stowes to abandon Harriet's father. Now an old man with a tendency to live in the past, he refused to accept the fact that Lane was on its last legs, and he still had spurts of enthusiasm when he clapped Hattie's husband on the back, promising miraculous improvements. To soften the parting, it was agreed that Professor Stowe would remain in Cincinnati one more year.

As to her father's personal welfare, Harriet thanked Heaven for a woman she detested. This was the third Mrs. Beecher, a former widow the Reverend had brought back from Boston following the death of his second wife. Though Mrs. Lydia Beecher continually exasperated her husband's grown children, Harriet and even Catharine trusted her to give him decent care until some feasible way to bring them both back East might be worked out.

Meanwhile, Harriet could not wait to leave Cincinnati herself. If her eighteen years there had seen her greatest happiness, they had also worn her into a pale and nerve-racked drudge. So as soon as she completed certain domestic arrangements, and no matter that she was pregnant again, she departed in April 1850, taking three children with her. Her husband and the two others would join her when they were able to, after she had rented and furnished a suitable house in Maine.

Uncle Tom

IT may seem surprising that Harriet even contemplated such a long and arduous trip on her own, in her condition, superintending three fretful youngsters plus a jumble of baggage. Indeed, anyone who saw this harried mother along her route was bound to pity her. For her journey was incredibly more taxing than travelers of the next century, flying the same distance in a matter of hours, could possibly realize.

Though railroads had, by 1850, mostly replaced horse-drawn conveyances, Harriet still had to change trains repeatedly, often in the middle of the night. Sometimes she had to spend a whole night in an isolated depot, her charges huddled around her, until the connecting train she wanted at last arrived. No shy, ineffectual female could have managed such an expedition.

In fact those eighteen years in Cincinnati had changed Harriet much more deeply than was visible. Not only had she learned to do whatever was necessary to keep her family afloat, while her husband belied his sturdy appearance with an inner helplessness in the face of crisis. Of immeasurably greater significance, she had also absorbed her own intense convictions about the major issue of the day—slavery.

In Cincinnati Harriet Beecher Stowe had lived practically as if she were encased by a shell around her own household. She made no friends with whom she would keep in touch; she participated not at all, following her marriage, in any community activity. Yet those owl eyes of hers had never ceased observing, nor had she failed to grasp the implications of what she saw.

Perhaps it had all started with her sister Catharine's account of their Aunt Mary's horrifying discovery, decades earlier, in the West Indies. This whispered tale of a white man's lust for a slave woman must have indelibly seared a sensitive girl brought up amid the high morality of a family like the Beechers. But, then, merely living in Cincinnati had to stir similar currents beneath the surface calm of an extraordinarily emotional and observant woman. For the city was situated on the Ohio River, directly opposite slave-owning Kentucky.

Once, as an unassuming teacher, Harriet had accompanied Mary Dutton on a weekend visit to the home of one of their pupils over in Kentucky. Though they stayed in a town, they had spent an afternoon at a plantation out in the countryside, where they were taken to see the slave quarters. That picture Harriet had etched onto her brain, complete to the smallest detail of a slave child turning cartwheels to make the white folks smile.

Throughout her Cincinnati years Harriet could not have avoided continually seeing posters and newspaper advertisements appealing for the return of runaway slaves. From a minister her father knew, who kept a light in his window that was visible from the Kentucky bank of the river, she had learned how some brave whites helped slaves to escape. During much of this period, however, most respectable opinion in the North condemned such efforts as unwarranted interference with the South. While slavery was considered morally wrong, even clergymen preached that it could be ended only gradually, by raising money to buy freedom for groups of families and resettle them in Africa. The Reverend Beecher himself had supported this colonization scheme.

By 1850, however, the ranks of those radicals who wanted to abolish slavery immediately had begun to swell. It was becoming almost respectable to be an abolitionist. Indeed, several of Harriet's clergymen brothers were now leaders in the antislavery cause—among them Edward, who had moved back to Boston with his own family.

Harriet stopped off at Edward's Boston home near the end of her journey eastward, so that she and her children could rest a few days before continuing to Maine. After dinner there one evening the conversation inevitably turned to the recent debate in Congress about adopting a stricter Fugitive Slave Law. Then Edward's wife addressed a fateful remark to her sister-in-law.

"Now, Hattie," Edward's wife said, "if I could use a pen as you can, I would write something that would make this whole nation feel what an accursed thing slavery is."

Upon hearing these words Harriet—not only worn from her trip, but also approaching the further strain of settling her family in a strange community and giving birth for the sixth time—rose from her chair. Her face was glowing with an exalted look that those present would not forget. "I will write something," she said. "I will if I live."

That winter, having been safely delivered of her baby Charley, Harriet was seated in church one Sunday morning when she suddenly saw a scene within her head that was unbelievably vivid. This picture showed her an elderly black man she instantly christened Uncle Tom, who was prayerfully forgiving his tormentors with his last breath before he died. It moved her so powerfully that she could hardly keep from weeping. As soon as she returned home, she grasped a pen and put down on paper what she had visualized.

Still, the pressures of daily existence prevented any further writing during the ensuing months. Not until Professor Stowe arrived in Brunswick and happened to pick up the sheets she had scrawled that Sunday did Harriet understand what she must do next. As her husband finished reading the fragment, with tears streaming down his face, he told her she *must* compose the beginning of the story for which this was the ending.

Yes, Harriet said, she felt that, too. And she had already formed a good many more pictures in her mind that she longed to start describing. Yet how could she possibly find the time for writing not merely a brief sketch but a whole book—unless she called on Catharine?

For Katy had promised to come if ever she was needed in just such circumstances, Harriet told her husband. No one else would assume so heavy a burden purely for love, she reminded him, and they could not possibly afford the wages of a capable housekeeper. So Professor Stowe had to agree, and a letter went off to Catharine.

True to her word, Sister Katy hurried eastward from Milwaukee, where she was organizing a new academy for teacher training. She arrived in Brunswick in August 1851. By then Harriet had already begun writing *Uncle Tom's Cabin.*

As was common practice in those days, Harriet had offered her work to a weekly newspaper, chapter by chapter, right at the outset. An antislavery publication called the *National Era* committed itself to taking about twelve installments, starting with the issue of June 5, 1851, and Harriet struggled to get the required chapters into the mail on time until her sister's arrival two months later. So Harriet welcomed Katy effusively.

Already Harriet, if not her editor, realized that her story had barely commenced. There would, in fact, be a new chapter every week until April 1, 1852. And the question of whether the *National Era*'s readers would remain interested in such a long tale had already been answered. Just before Catharine turned up, Harriet had failed to send one installment, and the paper went to press without Mrs. Stowe's contri-

Catharine Beecher in her old age.

Harriet Beecher Stowe in the early 1850s.

bution. Never had this narrowly circulated journal received such a flurry of letters as it got that week, demanding the continuation of *Uncle Tom*.

Catharine herself, having read and approved the story thus far, briskly assumed her own role. To Professor Stowe's horror, she pronounced that something had to be done to pay the family's accumulated bills, so she circularized her acquaintances, seeking boarding pupils for the parlor school she insisted on establishing. To preserve her brother-in-law from apoplexy, she advanced the necessary funds to provide classroom furniture out of the proceeds of her latest book.

She also relieved her sister immediately by taking full charge of the Stowe household. Almost as if Catharine felt that she herself was creating a literary masterpiece, she wrote to Sister Mary Perkins that she was "trying to get Uncle Tom out of the way." Thus: "At eight o'clock we are through with breakfast and prayers and then we send off Mr. Stowe and Harriet both to his room in the college. There was no other way to keep her out of family cares and quietly at work and since this plan is adopted she goes ahead finely."

Indeed Harriet did. By the time the last installment had been put into the mail, even its unpretentious author ventured to predict that publishing *Uncle Tom* as a book might now gain her the good black silk dress she had always wanted. Considering the interest the serial chapters had aroused, albeit in a minor paper devoted to the antislavery cause, Harriet thought this was not too much to expect. She had, incidentally, received three hundred dollars from the *National Era* for the entire manuscript.

Yet her personal estimate of her own stature was similarly humble. A year or two earlier the editor of a popular women's magazine had written to request a sketch of Mrs. Stowe's life for inclusion in a volume about female authors, and Harriet had replied that she was too uninteresting to merit such attention. "My sister, Catharine, has lived much more of a life and done more that can be told of than I whose course and employments have always been retired and domestic," Harriet informed this lady.

Then, virtually overnight, in the spring of 1852—when Harriet was nearly forty-one and Catharine had passed her fifty-first birthday— the status of both sisters changed drastically. For *Uncle Tom,* in book form, was an instant, phenomenal success. The first printing of five thousand copies sold out within two days. Soon enormous steam- powered presses were running, day and night, as the publisher, John P. Jewett, a small Boston firm, strove to meet the unprecedented demand. Within a year three hundred thousand copies had been sold in the United States, and more than a million additional in England and other countries.

So Harriet earned her good black silk dress. Although her husband, with his limited sense of business, had made a not particularly canny arrangement regarding her profit from the publication, she still received ten thousand dollars by that first summer. Nevertheless, Catharine fumed over what she considered an unfair contract and, convinced that her experience in this area entitled her to take a hand, she personally went to see the publisher. All she accomplished was to mortify Professor Stowe.

Stop her from making a fool of me, the Professor begged his wife. But Harriet sought, instead, to calm him. Catharine meant well, Har- riet reminded him, and could he not see that, suddenly, after so many years of being *the* Miss Beecher, it was hardly easy to be overshadowed by her younger sister?

Yet if Harriet amply demonstrated her sensitivity to Catharine's feelings, along with her own affection and gratitude, there can be no doubt that she also enjoyed the reversal that had occurred. Once, years earlier, she had written a sly little story about two sisters—the elder imposing and brilliant, the younger her inferior in all but a single respect. "It requires a very peculiar talent to be overlooked with a good grace," Hattie had written about the lesser sister, whom she had impishly named Kate. In that long-ago tale Kate grew up "almost eclipsed by the side of the peerless moon." Even so, it was the in- conspicuous Kate who won the handsomest man in town, though everybody had expected him to marry her big sister.

Whether the real Kate nourished any secret resentment over being displaced can only be guessed; if she did, she buried it so deeply that no sign of it ever emerged. For Catharine's behavior following the publication of *Uncle Tom* reflected the new situation in only one way. To further her own unceasingly optimistic projects, she made every possible use of her younger sister's sudden celebrity.

Just two months after the first printing of Harriet's book, Catharine proclaimed the start of a campaign she had been planning for several years. Having tried—and failed—to establish an effective national organization, under male leadership, that would found a network of training schools for teachers, now she wanted to achieve the same goal with an organization composed exclusively of women.

And the invitations she sent out announcing the group's first meeting reflected her plain recognition that Harriet had surpassed her as a public figure. They read: "Mrs. H. B. Stowe and Miss C. E. Beecher, in behalf of the American Woman's Educational Association, request your attendance . . ." At Catharine's request Harriet also penned a personal appeal beneath the printed message on dozens of cards: "Please invite your friends."

Understandably, though, Harriet could not devote unlimited time to Catharine's cause because other demands of many sorts increasingly claimed her attention. Even though the 1850s had no television interviewers to clamor for her appearance, she was sought after almost as urgently by the leaders of various branches of the antislavery movement. For *Uncle Tom's Cabin,* it quickly became apparent, was far more than just an immensely touching story, told with a series of unforgettable images, such as that of a slave woman, clutching her infant in her arms as she leaped across chunks of ice in the Ohio River, barely escaping her pursuers. The book also released a flood of emotion with great political implications in the South as well as the North.

To Southerners, Mrs. Stowe became the repulsive symbol of Northern hostility toward their whole way of life. Though Harriet had endeavored to paint a fair picture of slavery, showing its kindly aspects along with its cruelty, the South united in outrage over what it considered willful misrepresentation.

At the same time, Northern readers reacted with a similarly great surge of outrage against the system that could produce a vicious overseer like *Uncle Tom's* Simon Legree. Though Harriet, in her vain attempt to avoid antagonizing decent Southerners, had purposely made her villain a Vermonter by birth, this was easily ignored. Even moderate men and women, who had previously gone along with the idea that slavery should be considered solely the South's business, turned into abolitionists as they turned the pages of Mrs. Stowe's book. To see her in person, to shake her hand, became the ambition of thousands, an ambition that political-minded leaders in the antislavery ranks did their best to fulfill.

Thus Harriet, for all her modesty, became accustomed to sitting on the platform at meetings in Boston or New York. And she did not find the great bursts of applause that greeted her every appearance too unpleasant. Even across the Atlantic, *Uncle Tom* created such a sensation that committees were formed in every major English city for the purpose of circulating antislavery petitions to be ceremoniously presented to Mrs. Stowe. Thus, during the summer of 1853, the bemused Harriet and her proud Professor—now he liked to say he had always suspected his wife was a genius—set forth on a tour of Great Britain.

There the crowds that assembled at each of her stops rivaled those that, on other occasions, lined the streets for a glimpse of Queen Victoria. It was a heady experience, which imperceptibly changed the recipient of such adulation into a more forceful person. Still, Harriet remembered to write to Catharine about her own emotion at the sight of those rocks off the Irish coast marking the watery grave of Professor Fisher, and, in a lighter mood, she told her sister every detail of the ornate furnishings in the homes of the duchesses who sponsored various entertainments in her honor.

Meanwhile, Catharine was repeating her usual pattern of up-and-down involvement out in Wisconsin. No sooner had her remarkably zealous efforts produced a fine new school building in Milwaukee— which would remain one of the few enduring monuments to her decades of educational striving—than she became embroiled in dispute with the other trustees of the institution. Sadly, the focal point of the argument was Catharine's insistence on a separate building where she could make her own permanent home. For as she neared the age of sixty, she became increasingly aware that her rootless existence could not continue indefinitely.

Yet the male trustees of the school she had established were adamant in their refusal even to try to raise money for the kind of housing Catharine wanted. Why, they asked, could she not be quite comfortable with a private suite in the domestic science wing of the main structure? Typically, she would not compromise and, as a result, back she went to recuperate at a Massachusetts water cure. Then she resumed her wandering.

Having reached a somewhat venerable stage, Catharine had—it may seem surprising—less difficulty than ever in securing satisfactory hospitality wherever she wished to visit. Small slights had never troubled her, and now she began reaping unexpected rewards for her immunity to insult as well as her perseverance.

Some years earlier, for instance, when she had invited herself to the home of a nephew, there had been a problem. While Catharine was in the kitchen, conducting one of her culinary experiments, she had antagonized a maid, who then blurted a rude remark. Catharine had instantly fired her. Upon the nephew's return that evening, he was less than pleased to find his wife struggling to prepare supper. After learning what had happened, he strode upstairs, where his aunt was serenely working in her room on a book she was planning about the religious training of children.

"Aunt Catharine," the nephew declared, "your visit is over! Pack up your things. A hack will call for you first thing in the morning!"

But shortly after Catharine's Milwaukee failure, the same nephew happened to see his aging aunt seated on a Boston park bench. Remorse smote him for having evicted her from his home, and he hurried along, pretending not to have noticed her. But she recognized him. "Edward, do come and see the wonderful books I have just bought at that secondhand store on Tremont Street," she called. The young Edward, shamed by the memory of his own unkindness to an old woman who, after all, had such a good heart, heard himself saying, "Aunt Catharine, couldn't you arrange to come and pay us a visit right now?"

"Why, I should be delighted, Edward," she replied. And she spent the next two weeks at his home entirely placidly.

For Catharine's manner, as she grew older, did seem to mellow, making her strike other people as less abrasive. Or, perhaps, the same sort of outspoken comments that had sounded unbearably domineering when they had come from a youngish spinster now sounded intriguingly peppery coming from a quaint old maid.

Even so, Catharine relied more and more on the safe harbor that Harriet provided for months at a time. Since Professor Stowe had stayed only briefly in Maine because he received a superior offer from the theological seminary in Andover, Massachusetts, this pleasant community just north of Boston became Catharine's principal headquarters during the late 1850s. Much to the awe of Andover's citizenry, the Professor's famous wife had caused such extensive remodeling of an old stone cottage that it almost resembled a castle. Here the two sisters, in the intervals between their busy schedules elsewhere, again enjoyed the special intimacy they had shared so long ago in Litchfield.

Another Stowe tragedy actually brought them closer than ever because of the memories it invoked. In 1856 Harriet finished her second antislavery novel, *Dred*—another huge success, although it would later be almost forgotten. Once the book had been issued in the United States, its author decided to visit England again to prevent the sort of literary piracy that had lost her a fortune when unauthorized editions of *Uncle Tom* had flooded Europe. Also, the prospect of increasing her aristocratic acquaintanceship abroad somehow did not dismay this Puritan daughter.

49

On her return to Andover she rejoiced at having her family surrounding her, except that her favorite son Henry, now a freshman at
Dartmouth College, had not been able to welcome her owing to his
heavy burden of examinations. Less than a week later, a terrible telegram arrived: Henry, while out swimming, had drowned in the Connecticut River.

Suddenly the same sort of religious torture that had afflicted
Catharine after the death of Professor Fisher more than thirty years
earlier reduced Harriet to just the shadow of her newly assured self.
No matter that her own youthful struggle with her father's harsh
dogma had gradually given her a less rigid personal faith; it was almost
as if an inner demon had taken possession of her. Suppose her darling
Henry was, this very instant, burning in hell!

But if there was a certain similarity in the circumstances of Henry's
death and Professor Fisher's, Harriet had the advantage of Catharine's

*A portrait of the Beecher family about 1855 by the noted photographer
Mathew Brady. The Reverend Beecher is seated in the middle, with
Catharine on his right. Mary and Harriet are seated at his left.*

warm consolation. Indeed, Catharine's reliving of her own youthful suffering made it possible, at last, for her to cast off the whole harsh creed of her father—and join the more liberal Episcopal Church. Harriet soon followed her example, finding the spiritual solace she craved.

Furthermore, Harriet had another way of easing her mind and heart. With her imaginative talent, she combined the tragedies of her son and her sister's intended husband into a work of fiction that she called *The Minister's Wooing*. On its surface, the novel's story differed substantially from the events on which it was based. It told of a deeply religious girl, crushed by the drowning of her betrothed, who, in time, let herself be convinced it was her duty to marry an austere clergyman who loved her, but a week before the impending wedding, the girl's handsome sailor miraculously reappeared to save her from sacrificing herself—and assure a happy ending. Yet the book's real claim to literary merit lay in its moving passages of religious questioning by its heroine and its hero's mother. It is obvious that both these figures were inspired by Catharine because many of their most thoughtful phrases can be found, word for word, in letters she had written to her father at the height of her anguish over the death of her own intended husband.

Less traumatically, Catharine and Harriet also cooperated on another literary project that gave them both a great deal of pleasure. By now their father and his third wife had joined the rest of the family in the East and, even if the Reverend Beecher's mind sometimes wandered, he cherished the aim of putting down the story of his life for the benefit of posterity. Yet he could no longer concentrate long enough to do the job himself. The youngest of his first wife's sons—the Reverend Charles Beecher—assumed the task of sifting through old sermons and serving as editor of the whole opus, but it was sisters Katy and Hattie who put their heads together over chapters of family reminiscence that made the resulting two volumes a matchless document in American history.

While this private celebration of the past was giving the sisters such a sense of unity, Harriet's position as the high priestess of the antislavery movement had a far greater divisive effect. Besides *Uncle Tom*, her subsequent writings and appearances unquestionably incited an increasing hostility between the two parts of the United States. Of course, there were a multitude of other factors that contributed toward the outbreak of shooting in 1861, following the election of the former Illinois Congressman Abraham Lincoln as President of the United States.

But when Mrs. Stowe went to Washington a year or so after the firing on Fort Sumter, President Lincoln greeted her at the White House with a rather gory pleasantry: "So this is the little lady who made this big war."

Afterward

NOT even a Southern mother could have denied that the Civil War brought Harriet Beecher Stowe a particularly sharp and lasting personal misery. Though her own little Charley was too young to do more than play at being a soldier, her only other surviving son suffered a pitiful fate after he left the Harvard Medical School to enlist in the First Massachusetts Volunteers. Struck by a shell fragment during the Battle of Gettysburg, Fred did not die—immediately.

But even though his head wound seemed almost healed, following long months of hospitalization, Fred emerged with no willpower and he became a drunkard. For a family that staunchly supported the temperance movement, the sight of Fred reeling around their neighborhood had to cause acute pain. Yet every type of cure his parents hopefully arranged ended in another drunken spree until, in 1871, they encouraged Fred to sign aboard a ship bound for South America. As a sailor, they thought, he would be safe from temptation. The vessel's first stop, however, was San Francisco, where the Stowes' unfortunate son disappeared. And, despite pressing efforts, no trace of him was ever discovered.

A singular quality of Harriet's helped her beyond measure throughout these years while her formerly upstanding son was causing her so much anguish. It was her ability to live on different levels, almost simultaneously. Thus, at the height of her wretchedness over Fred's falling apart, she never ceased writing diligently, producing some of her finest New England stories, along with a stream of more prosy newspaper and magazine articles. For she needed every penny she could earn in order to build—at last—the castle of her dreams.

On the banks of that same river in Hartford where, as a schoolgirl, she had strolled with Georgiana May and confessed her ambitious fantasy, Harriet in the middle of the 1860s created an astounding structure—"with eight gables," as she proudly informed a newer friend. But her fairy-tale architecture did not lend itself to the installation of the up-to-date plumbing she also required. The bursting of frozen water pipes, therefore, became a frequent occurrence during the cold New England winters. One night a torrent descended directly over Professor Stowe's bed, impelling him to leap up and shout: "Oh, yes, all the modern conveniences! Shower baths while you sleep!"

Indeed, the expense of the whole establishment caused the Professor immense anxiety. Being of an age and temperament to enjoy the prospect of just reading all day, leaving his pile of books only to savor ample meals, Harriet's roly-poly husband had been quite willing to retire from Andover when she had broached the subject. Still, he had failed to anticipate his wife's extravagance, or the impossibility of keeping the castle sufficiently warm to suit his old bones. "It's no use!" he kept grumbling. "Nothing can stop our going to the poorhouse!"

Nor had the Professor anticipated how much of his sister-in-law Catharine's company the move to Hartford would oblige him to endure, for this city of her first success as an educational pioneer retained a special aura in her memories. Moreover, many of her former students, now grandmothers, had fond memories of her, too, besides being in a position to help her on new projects. Ever the optimist, never deterred by past failures, she was nearing the ripe age of seventy with an undiminished fountain of ideas—and what better site could there be from which to spout them than Harriet's castle?

Catharine also counted on Harriet's husband for guidance in her own unending process of adding to her store of knowledge. And Professor Stowe had no objection at all when she consulted him as a superior authority. In small doses, administered not too often, and in circumstances where no expenditure of money need be discussed, he actually liked Kate.

Yet he could not tolerate a steady diet of Catharine's tart advice, especially after she assumed the mission of reforming his eating habits. When she summoned the effrontery to lecture him on his "morbid" craving for food, going so far as to suggest that he limit himself *greatly* by consuming just one small meal a day, the Professor did not hide his disgust from his wife.

Harriet, without anyone's taking formal notice, had, in effect, become the head of the Stowe family. So it was she who proposed what surely seemed the solution to several problems at one fell swoop. Since a touch of rheumatism was afflicting several of her fingers—a serious matter for the literary support of an elaborate household, in an era before any machine had displaced human handwriting—she suggested a winter trip by boat down along the eastern coast to an area of northern Florida that she had heard was delightfully springlike, even in February. Catharine, meanwhile, would visit Brother Edward in Brooklyn.

Not far from Jacksonville, Harriet and her husband found a cottage in an orange grove that suited them both ideally. Here she could write painlessly and uninterruptedly; he could doze in the sunshine when he tired of reading. For a time it also seemed possible that Fred might recover by healthfully spending his days supervising former slaves in

55

creating a thriving farm. Although this effort failed, Fred's parents still found the Florida climate so congenial that, during the next two decades, they went there late every autumn and stayed until winter had positively departed from New England.

By now Catharine no longer had the energy for long trips or for providing much in the way of housekeeping assistance to Harriet, even if she still needed such aid. But Harriet's own twin daughters, impressively stylish as they had grown, both had uneventfully gone beyond the age when most girls married, without finding any reason to leave home. Of the seven children born to the Stowes, only their high-strung Georgiana and amiable young Charley would give them grandchildren to cherish in their declining years. Considering the price of fame, though, it was the twins to whom Harriet owed the most.

Nearing their fifteenth birthday when *Uncle Tom* had thrust their mother into the limelight, young Hattie and Eliza had almost imperceptibly begun shielding her in many ways. As the years passed, they became extremely efficient secretaries—and housekeepers—and yet they managed to divide the burdens so that neither felt oppressed. Thus they set up a system in the late 1860s whereby one of them took full charge in Florida, while the other relaxed, and in Hartford the situation was reversed.

Despite their identical appearance, Eliza and her sister Hattie had quite different personalities, which diverted a new neighbor in Hartford. To his private notebook, he confided his own names for them: "Soft Soap" and "Hellfire." If these seem unusually descriptive, nobody who knew Sam Clemens would have been surprised; to the world at large, the Stowes' neighbor was better known as Mark Twain.

Actually, it was the Stowes who had moved and thereupon become the sharers of a common backyard boundary with the Clemens family. For after six years even Harriet was forced to admit that her castle had been a costly mistake. Besides its own flaws, its location proved increasingly unhealthful because the formerly picturesque little river it overlooked had become polluted by encroaching factories. Giving up her attempt to make a girlhood dream come true, she bought a somewhat more modest house in a select community just beyond the city limits, where she probably would have settled to start with if her streak of the Beecher weakness for grandiosity had not temporarily overcome her Beecher common sense.

By concentrating as we have on Catharine and Harriet, we have lost touch with the rest of their relatives, but now it is necessary to catch up briefly with two of them. The youngest of the Reverend Beecher's four daughters—Isabella—has appeared only anonymously, in our mere mention of her birth in our first chapter. Belle, sent East from Cincinnati when her mother's health began failing, had not only lived with her sister Mary Perkins during her schooldays, she also married one of her Hartford brother-in-law's younger associates, a descendant of Connecticut's eminent Hooker clan.

Reading her husband's legal tomes, Isabella Hooker became infuriated by their attitude toward women. To Sister Kate's horror, Sister Belle turned into Connecticut's leading advocate of the radical woman's rights movement. Founded in 1848 with the aim of gaining full citizenship for the nation's females, its main goal was obtaining the right to vote.

Belle's husband was not nearly so upset by her unladylike speech-making as Sister Kate was. Part of the explanation for his tolerance may have been the fact that his wife was the only one of the Beecher girls who had been blessed with a pretty face. In any case, it was Belle's adoring mate who started an exclusive new community on one hundred acres of unspoiled farmland at the edge of Hartford, where about a dozen congenial families gradually built substantial red brick mansions surrounded by broad and shady lawns.

Here Catharine and Harriet played uncounted games of croquet during the summers around 1870. Also, Catharine appointed herself the mistress of ceremonies at various wholesome amusements, including amateur musicales. She made a Sunday night hymn-singing memorable when somebody proposed an anthem with the chorus: "I am nothing, Lord, oh nothing—Thou art all, all!" For Miss Beecher shook her head. "I don't wish to sing that," she said. "I am *not* nothing!"

Still we must admit that this presumption of Catharine's could also be exasperating. In 1870 she unwisely took on a task that quickly proved too much for her, letting herself be prevailed on to resume the active direction of her original Hartford Female Seminary. It was losing money and all but defunct, having been unable to compete with newer free public high schools that were offering girls a similar program. For her pioneering curriculum had, during the nearly fifty years since she had introduced it, become generally adopted. So Catharine's attempt to revive the seminary ended after less than six months with an angry dispute between her and the trustees about the cost of a new furnace.

This failure of hers followed other similar, if less public, defeats. With her typically high-handed manner, Catharine had informed her Hooker brother-in-law that she wished to buy the *whole* of the parcel of land adjoining Mrs. Stowe's property for the headquarters of her American Woman's Educational Association. How much would this cost? John Hooker tersely informed her, "We should ask one hundred thousand dollars." Of course, such a sum went far beyond Catharine's means.

Possibly, though, John Hooker had purposely aimed to punish Catharine because of her attitude toward his wife's suffragist activities. "My soul is cast down," Catharine had written to a prominent clergyman in New Haven, "at the ignorance and mistaken zeal of my poor Sister Belle and her co-agitators. Can you not lend a pen to show . . . how much *moral* power is gained by taking a subordinate place?"

Yet the Beecher family cannot be deprived of its extraordinary complications. Within a few years Catharine changed her mind about woman suffrage, at least to a limited extent. Perhaps the ballot would not be harmful, she conceded, if it was limited to educated females who were unmarried but owned property upon which they paid taxes.

Again, we of the late twentieth century are bound to admire Catharine more for what she did than what she said—and during the great Beecher scandal that erupted in the middle of the 1870s, Catharine as an old woman showed a doughty spirit that must be respected. So did Harriet.

At this late stage in their story, we must—finally—meet the most famous Beecher of them all. Even before Harriet blazed into prominence with *Uncle Tom's Cabin,* the brother who was two years her junior already rivaled the vastly popular circus impresario P. T. Barnum as possibly the greatest celebrity on the American scene. More than just a preacher, the Reverend Henry Ward Beecher was a public figure of unmatched standing.

For Brother Henry had not merely an amazingly warm and ringing voice, but his message of God's love was just what optimistic Americans wished to receive. He lectured all over the country; tourists by the thousands crowded his huge church in Brooklyn. At the end of the Civil War in 1865, President Lincoln had chosen him to officiate when the Stars and Stripes were symbolically raised again at Fort Sumter in Charleston's harbor.

Less than ten years later, this most eminent moral leader stood in a courtroom, accused of committing adultery with the wife of one of his principal aides. It was a scandal beyond compare in the nation's history. Catharine and Harriet vigorously upheld their brother's honor while newspapers everywhere printed uncountable columns of gossip and testimony connected with the sensational case.

Despite Henry's fervent insistence on his innocence—which the court would uphold, although doubts still remain among some historians—his ordeal brought a division in the ranks of his brothers and sisters. The second Mrs. Beecher's three offspring, for various reasons, decided that Henry was probably guilty, but the children of his own mother unanimously supported him. By now Sister Belle, leading the anti-Henry camp, was at least slightly unhinged on the subject of her own divine mission to exalt womankind, and she felt called upon to take the pulpit in Henry's church, there to denounce him for mistreating a blameless female. Lest this threat be carried out, Harriet spent week after week in Brooklyn, ready to grab Belle and somehow silence her if it became necessary.

Meanwhile, the seventy-five-year-old Catharine conducted her own plot behind the scenes. Because of the suffragist connections of the woman who allegedly had been seduced, Susan B. Anthony and other leaders in the cause were all telling the newspapers about Henry's guilt. One day Catharine cornered a group, inveigled them into a hansom cab, and, ordering the driver to go back and forth in the park, out of the range of prying eyes, the irate Miss Beecher lectured her unwilling companions for several hours.

If her plotting had little effect, at least it demonstrated her undiminished loyalty and determination. Yet the effort exhausted her to the extent that she realized she might not have much time left. Already she had finished what she clearly understood must be her last two books. One was a revised version of her most successful domestic science treatise, which her publisher had been reluctant to accept.

After all, he said, hadn't Miss Beecher, ah, lost touch with the latest trends in domestic management? Catharine, to convince him that the book would attract readers, suggested an arrangement harking back to the day when her unknown sister had been helped by *her* importance. Sadly but realistically, like Harriet's first geography text, *The American Woman's Home* bore two names on its green cloth cover: "By Catharine E. Beecher and Harriet Beecher Stowe." During its preparation, throughout a Hartford summer, Harriet actually had contributed a few passages from some of her magazine articles, though the bulk of the work was Catharine's. In her final literary effort, however, Catharine once more stood squarely on her own, her *Educational Reminiscences* presenting a nearly serene summation of her long career.

Then there remained only a private task that she set herself before her strength inevitably failed. Alone, an old unmarried lady still wearing a gold engagement ring on her arthritic finger, Catharine journeyed to the home of Professor Fisher's nephew, where the letters she had sent her intended husband half a century earlier were packed away. Upon her arrival, the trunk was unlocked and she sat for hours beside the fireplace in the guest room, reading the loving words she had written so long ago—and then tossing them into the flames.

Catharine also destroyed Professor Fisher's letters to her. Of course, her wish to preserve her deepest feelings from the prying eyes of strangers was entirely justified. Yet Catharine also prevented future generations from ever seeing the most appealing side of her strong personality.

Instead, the image of her that would survive her lacked the human warmth that might have saved her from the fate of being forgotten. As it was, following the destruction of her love letters, Catharine almost peacefully awaited death. Though many members of her family, especially her father—who had died, at eighty-eight, in 1863— had worried over how she would cope on her own with the rigors of old age, she had no such worries herself. She had spent whatever she earned, mostly to further her causes, trusting that somehow she would be helped when she needed help. And she was.

It was the wife of Catharine's brother Thomas in the upstate New York city of Elmira who provided the solution. Since she and her husband lived directly across the road from a water cure that Catharine had frequented, Julia knew what she was undertaking when she said, "I think there are worse afflictions in the world than the care of an old Christian woman who has at least tried to do good all her life and needs someone's kind attention till the Lord calls her home. I am not going to worry about that."

So, in 1877, with Catharine as old as the century, Julia welcomed her for as long as she would stay. From Florida there arrived a cheerful letter addressed to Sister Katy. "I am relieved and glad to think of you at home at last with Brother Tom," Harriet wrote. "Too many years have passed over your head for you to be wandering like a trunk without a label."

In Elmira Catharine organized sewing classes for girls from local workmen's families, she visited the invalids at the neighboring water cure, and, no matter that her handwriting grew ever more wavering, she kept writing letters. ". . . my life has been a very happy one," she told one acquaintance. And, "I am in correspondence with the best leaders of popular education . . . and I hope to be in Philadelphia in about ten days," she informed another.

But two days after that last hope had been expressed, on May 12, 1878, four months before her seventy-eighth birthday, Catharine died in her sleep at the home of her Elmira brother. Then her favorite brother Edward came from his own retirement in Brooklyn to officiate at her funeral. Unfortunately, Harriet could not be present because Professor Stowe was ailing.

Catharine's death was marked by newspapers in many cities with tributes such as few women had received. "It has been the fortune of very few women in this country to exercise a degree of influence at all comparable with that of Catharine Beecher," said the Boston *Daily Advertiser,* while the Hartford *Courant* headed its two-column editorial about her career: A NOTABLE FIGURE AMONG THE WOMEN OF HER TIME.

Nevertheless, she left no institution to keep her memory alive, like Mary Lyon's Mount Holyoke College. And her strong opinions about woman's proper sphere would find ever fewer supporters, even among the conservative-minded. With a manner that had made many people dislike her or ridicule her during her lifetime, she could hardly be expected to seem more appealing after her death.

And yet, after nearly a century of almost complete neglect, Catharine Beecher would stir new interest when the study of women's history began to be pursued widely during the 1960s. Regardless of what she preached, the fact that this woman had proved it was possible for an unmarried female to live an independent life made her suddenly more interesting to a new generation of feminists. Indeed, her insistence that women be given better training for their domestic role would be reassessed as "domestic feminism" by a leading professor of women's studies.*

Still, it is Catharine's continuing influence on her sister Harriet that we have been examining, and one last instance of this remains to be noted. In 1870, while Catharine had been spending the summer in Hartford with the Stowes, an editor was becoming impatient for a story Harriet had promised to provide for his magazine. But Harriet, approaching the age of sixty herself, found it increasingly difficult to meet deadlines. Catharine, with her long experience of prodding her young sister, took up her own pen to advise the editor on his best course: "Now if you will write as encouragingly as you can . . . and show how well you can manage if she *does not* be ready for the first of November—it will make it almost sure she will be ready."

After Catharine's death there was no such pressure to stimulate Harriet. Perhaps merely by coincidence, her last book was published in the year Catharine died—or is it possible that her eldest sister's departure removed a necessary spur? In any case, Harriet survived Catharine by eighteen years, physically in good health almost to the end. Her mind, however, gradually drifted into a private world of her own until, in the months following her husband's death in 1886, she slipped entirely into a peaceful second childhood.

Watched over by her conscientious twins, she gathered little bunches of flowers in her Hartford garden, she sat singing to herself during bad weather, and she retained no connection whatever with the changing scene beyond her own home. When, at last, she died at the age of eighty-five, on July 1, 1896, she had long since become just a figure from the past to the millions who read her lengthy obituary notices. Nevertheless, *her* fame was secure.

---

*Kathryn Kish Sklar of the University of California at Los Angeles in *Catharine Beecher: A Study in American Domesticity*, published by the Yale University Press in 1973.

· II ·

Charlotte Cushman and Susan Cushman Muspratt

A Tomboy Grows Up

I was born a tomboy. My earliest recollections are of dolls' heads cracked open to see what they were thinking about; I was possessed by the idea that dolls could and did think. I had no faculty for making dolls' clothes. But their furniture I could make skillfully. I could do anything with tools.

THUS did Charlotte Cushman start her only attempt to tell the story of her life—and she deftly sketched a picture of a little girl who must have caused much head-shaking back when young females were all supposed to excel at sewing, not sawing. Still, her own brief memoir left out some basic facts regarding her family, besides offering only a few hints concerning their feelings. To understand her and her youngest sister Susan, it is necessary to begin with the *Mayflower*.

Among the passengers aboard that famous ship that brought the first Pilgrims from England in 1620 was the unmarried daughter of an Isaac Allerton. The first Cushman to reach America did not arrive until 1621 on the *Fortune,* the second ship bearing New England settlers. But Thomas Cushman married Mary Allerton, thereby bequeathing all his descendants the right to claim *Mayflower* ancestry.

In Massachusetts, as the centuries passed, such a *Mayflower* connection became increasingly prized as a symbol of the closest approximation to aristocracy on this side of the Atlantic. Nevertheless, the New World differed from the Old in its up-and-down mobility. Though the original Thomas Cushman had really been rather high and mighty, serving forty-three years as an elder of the original Plymouth church, some branches of his family declined. Six generations later, on a scrabbly farm outside Plymouth, a boy named Elkanah Cushman found himself a penniless orphan at the age of thirteen.

He hiked to Boston and, with a spurt of the drive that had motivated his forebears, managed to become a partner in the firm of Topliffe and Cushman, operating a small warehouse on the city's Long Wharf. When he was forty-six, a widower and the father of two grown children, he married a second time. The following year, on July 23, 1816, Charlotte Cushman was born.

Even before she was old enough to frame the thought, Charlotte knew that women sometimes took charge if men failed. She learned this from Granny Babbit, her mother's mother, who lived with them in their narrow three-story house on a cobbled street lined with similar dwellings of families neither rich nor poor. Years earlier, Granny Babbit had married a lawyer in the town of Sturbridge, also a man of notable connections; among his relatives were Winthrops and Sargents and Saltonstalls, all great names in Massachusetts history. Yet her husband loved music better than law. Playing on his fiddle from sunrise to sunset, he made so little money that she defied the prevailing belief in female obedience. She took her three children and set off on her own for Boston.

Until her two sons were old enough to find work, she eked out a meager existence running a boardinghouse. Both boys were establishing themselves in the city's shipping trade by the time her youngest child—her daughter, Mary Eliza Babbit—attracted a suitor more than twice her age. Mary Eliza was just twenty-two, earning a pittance for giving a few pupils singing lessons, when she met and married Elkanah Cushman.

During the next decade Mary Eliza had no cause to demonstrate that she, too, possessed her mother's exceptional spirit of independence. Within a year she gave birth to Charlotte, then two years later she had a son, Charlie, who kept her busy domestically. But only after the lapse of another four years, on the birth of her second daughter, Susan—on March 17, 1822—did Mary Eliza feel the full flowering of maternal love. For Susan was a beautiful child.

Mary Eliza was no beauty herself. She had a broad, square face by no means unappealing, mainly because of her alert blue eyes, but nobody had ever given her the sort of admiration pretty girls take for granted. Somehow her lack of such attention made her value it immensely, which would have a profound effect on her daughters. For Charlotte was no beauty, either.

It may seem that a mother who had suffered pangs over her own plain appearance would have a special sympathy for a daughter who looked like her. But mothers as well as other people are not easily predictable. In fact, Mary Eliza treated Charlotte rather coldly, even prior to Susan's arrival, which the sensitive and yet unusually sociable and sturdy little Lottie reacted to by seeking warmth elsewhere. She found it, right at home, from Granny Babbit:

> I remember sitting at her feet on a little stool and hearing
> her sing a song of the period, in which she delighted me by
> the most perfect imitation of every creature belonging to the
> barnyard. She was also remarkably clever, bright and
> witty. . . .

Charlotte, having these same qualities, along with her mother's broad, square face, happily devoted herself to copying Granny's tricks of sounding like a cow or sow. "Mooo-oooo," she practiced, holding her breath, and, hilariously, "Oink-oink-oink!" Only after Susan's birth, when Lottie was nearly six, did she gradually realize from her mother's effusive praise of the baby's every smile that this dainty little sister had a way of winning approval that she herself could not hope to equal. But Lottie hated to be considered inferior, so she bossed Susan at every opportunity and did what she liked best herself, regardless of her mother's frowns.

On the docks Charlotte boldly joined the boys in playing hide-and-seek among the mountains of packing cases. She even took the lead in the dangerous game of leaping back and forth from the wharf to the swaying deck of some vessel tied up to be loaded or unloaded. One day she lost her footing and tumbled into the icy water; she was thrashing in panic when a man came running to rescue her. Shivering and dripping, she was carried to her father's warehouse. There the only dry clothes were a man's jacket and overalls, in which ridiculously oversize garments she was obliged to walk home to her mother.

Mary Eliza greeted her with an outburst of anger that softened, though, as soon as Charlotte sneezed. For if this mother could not help regretting her elder daughter's unfeminine brashness, no more than she could help favoring her sweet, docile Susan, still she tried to do her duty. So she nursed Charlotte through the sneezing and wheezing that followed her escapade, without another word about punishment. Indeed, in the series of difficulties that soon overtook the family, Mary Eliza leaned increasingly on her vigorous eldest child.

First, Granny Babbit became ill. When a tumor was discovered, the physician they summoned gave no hope, and for months Granny lay upstairs suffering. Then it was Charlotte who offered her own comic imitations—of Miss Graves, their sour spinster neighbor, or even of their exceptionally solemn young parson—in an effort to relieve the sickroom misery. From this childhood vigil during the lingering death of her dearest friend on earth, Charlotte acquired one of the few fears that would remain with her always, her dread of cancer.

After Granny died, a new birth created a joyous interlude. Mary Eliza, in 1825, when Charlotte was nine, had a second son, Augustus, who soon became his eldest sister's particular favorite. Though her brother Charlie was only two years her junior and her constant play-mate, Charlie had no spark of fun or the kind of mind that popped out with embellishments for her own continuous improvising. In fact, he was as dull and quiet as any boy of normal intelligence could be. But Gus, even as an infant, showed a quick humor that marked him as quite a different sort of brother. Charlotte, amusing him with her repertoire of barnyard oinks, very early concluded that he would be the cleverest of their parents' children.

It is easy to guess that the ineffectual Charlie took after their father, because, in the same year Augustus was born, Elkanah Cushman lost his business. Somehow his partner acquired full control of the firm's assets, leaving Elkanah bankrupt at the age of fifty-six. It was a disgrace from which he could not recover. Although he lived another fifteen years, he retreated to the fireside of the married daughter his first wife had given him becoming just a shadowy memory thereafter for his second family.

So Mary Eliza confronted an emergency such as the prevailing opinion of the day simply assumed was impossible. How could a wife of thirty-two, with four young children, be in danger of starving? Surely even if her husband was in some way incapacitated, she would be helped by other relatives. But Mary Eliza's brothers could provide only limited assistance.

With their aid, she moved to a shabby neighborhood and put up placards welcoming boarders. Showing that she certainly could, if necessary, muster something like Granny Babbit's brave independence, she cooked and scrubbed and stirred boiling cauldrons of laundry in her effort to keep her children from the awful fate of an orphan asylum. Never for an instant, though, did she accept such drudgery as her permanent lot, or as the best her children should expect themselves.

After all, they had *Mayflower* kin, besides dozens of other eminent if distant cousins. With such good blood, she kept drumming into them, they could not remain at this lowest rung of society more than just temporarily. But while Mary Eliza's ambitions went no further than merely regaining the moderately comfortable status she had enjoyed and lost, her eldest daughter, by the age of thirteen, already was aiming higher.

That was the year Charlotte left school to help her mother support them all. If this daughter had been less ambitious, she might have gone to work hemming shirts for a few pennies an hour, practically the only occupation open to poor girls who still wished to be considered respectable. Or, without too much loss of reputation, she might have entered another household as more or less a servant; in this case, it would be generally understood that she was keeping an eye open for a likely husband of her own while she spent a couple of years assisting an overburdened wife. But Charlotte detested sewing and endured domestic chores impatiently. She loved singing—and her voice was unusually rich and true—so why could she not seek a musical career?

Mary Eliza, despite all her stress on propriety, hesitated about forbidding Charlotte to think of such an uncommon calling. For Boston, around 1830, had numerous new churches of the Unitarian persuasion that were striving to demonstrate their difference from the austere old Puritanism by the glory of their choirs. Since the Cushmans were Unitarians, Charlotte's mother felt it was quite permissible to sing in public, and earn a small fee if the performance was part of a church service. Indeed, she knew a family whose daughters sang in various choirs and were much in demand. But did Charlotte's voice entitle her to vie with those talented sisters?

Though Mary Eliza had always been fond of singing herself and had even given lessons before her marriage, she was concerned lest her motherly partiality confuse her judgment. So she sought advice from an old acquaintance of her husband's, a retired sea captain with musical leanings who had invested his savings in a piano factory started by a man named Chickering. At this factory, while her mother kept nervously wringing her hands, the thirteen-year-old Charlotte for the first time in her life faced a critical audience.

Having recently grown like a weed, topping the five-foot mark by a full five inches, she felt as gawky as a giraffe, and a terrible lump filled her throat. But the instant she started to sing, a marvelous elation banished her fright. Then when Charlotte finished her song, the former sea captain nodded with a kindly smile. Aye, her voice had promise, he said. She ought to come often and use one of his pianos for practicing.

During the next several years Charlotte did so almost daily and, one way or another, she also took lessons that were more rigorous than her mother could provide. At the same time, the youthful Miss Cushman became a regular singer in a church that paid her barely as much as she could have made stitching shirt collars. Still, the experience was beyond price because of the sermons there, which she raptly heeded. Soon the Reverend Ralph Waldo Emerson would give up preaching in favor of writing, but by then an ungainly, eager, blue-eyed girl who sang at his services had absorbed just what she needed from his discourses on self-reliance.

At eighteen, Charlotte no longer argued when Mary Eliza fretted over her notion of possibly someday singing opera music in a theater. Just as this daughter had outdistanced her mother in height—Charlotte was thankful, though, that, having reached five and a half feet, she had stopped shooting upward—now she depended more on her own judgment than on her mother's. Beneath her assured manner, which Mary Eliza deferred to while persisting in querulous protests, Charlotte would never stop wishing she might please her mother as much as the quiet and delicate Susan did. No matter, Charlotte listened to her mother's warnings, then did precisely as she herself thought best.

Somebody had to save their fatherless family from disaster, she felt. Her mother could not continue working like a slave, keeping boarders fed. Her brother Charlie, it was clear, lacked the gumption to assume responsibility himself. Of course, pretty little Susan would meekly go on drying dishes until some young fellow claimed her as his bride.

And, without adequate schooling, even her cherished Gus, when he got older, could never amount to much.

So Charlotte jutted out her chin to discourage the two upstanding young men—coincidentally, both were also named Charlie—who were hanging around her with the hope that she might suddenly behave more like a proper young lady. Instead, she made up her mind that, sooner or later, she herself would find a way to sustain her whole tribe. It happened even sooner than she had hoped.

About three months before she turned nineteen, an English opera star named Mary Anne Wood arrived in Boston for a limited engagement, and she visited the Chickering factory seeking a suitably melodious piano to accompany her. While she was there, she asked if anyone could recommend a contralto singer in the area who could harmonize with her own soprano on a short program of duets. Charlotte, many years later, would calmly describe her trial at the English prima donna's hotel suite:

> Mrs. Wood received me very kindly, and I rehearsed with her, "As it fell upon a day." She seemed to be much impressed by the voice, for she immediately sent up stairs to ask Mr. Wood to come down. He came, and I sang again, and at the end of the duet they both seemed much pleased, and both assured me that such a voice properly cultivated would lead me to any height of fortune I coveted.

If the mature Charlotte could take such a matter-of-fact attitude toward the first real test of her soaring hopes, the young Charlotte was far from serene during the next hectic weeks. For Mr. Wood, as his wife's manager, proposed an innovation bound to draw large audiences. Beyond Mrs. Wood's announced program, he scheduled another opera—Mozart's *The Marriage of Figaro*—with one of the main supporting roles to be sung by Boston's own Miss Cushman.

Not only were American singers of operatic caliber a rarity then, but Charlotte's youth made her a subject of intense interest to the local newspapers. Amid a buzz of patriotic excitement, because the

United States was about to show Europe that it, too, could produce a prima donna, Charlotte rehearsed day and night. From what she would tell friends long afterward, she barely was able to hide her terror as her debut came rushing upon her.

On the evening of April 8, 1835, Charlotte stepped out onto the stage of Boston's Tremont Theatre, dressed in an elaborate gown befitting her impersonation of the Countess Almaviva. As Mr. Wood had anticipated, she faced a full house comprised more of well-wishers than of critics disposed to condemn her inexperience. But even though the audience was ready to encourage her by excusing blemishes, as one critic wrote, "there was no such necessity."

Not that she scored a complete triumph, despite the thunderous applause and the bouquets of flowers that rewarded her as the curtain descended. One of the more cautious of Boston's writers about cultural events told the readers of the *Daily Atlas* that Miss Cushman "was well received" even if . . .

> . . . the lady evinced much timidity at her first entrance, and was not wholly assured throughout the piece. She did not pitch her voice quite high enough for the house, and she put rather less energy into her part than it would bear. Then she did not know what to do with her train [of her gown], and this is all the fault we could find in her.

Otherwise, the captious *Atlas* critic referred to the generous statement by Mrs. Wood that "this young person" had a voice naturally superior to her own and needed only further training. The *Atlas* added:

> Without going that length, we are bold to think that it is extremely powerful in its high notes and sweet in its lower ones, and is under command to a degree that is astonishing in so young a performer. We do not say it cannot be improved by study and practice, but we do assert, without fear

of contradiction, that even at present it is far superior to that of any American performer who has trod our boards.

So Charlotte—if not her mother—had ample reason for rejoicing. Because Boston's verdict, on balance, was so extremely heartening, Mr. Wood came forth with a further plan that seemed to surpass any dream. After Boston his wife was booked to sing for six whole months in the glamorous metropolis, more than a thousand miles southward, of New Orleans. Would Miss Cushman consider joining their company and playing several major roles there?

To Charlotte, no possible objection made any sense, yet Mary Eliza raised one obstacle after another. Of course, the distance between Massachusetts and Louisiana was infinitely greater in those days before even telegraph wires connected the country's vast expanse. But geographical miles distressed Charlotte's mother less than the immeasurable other distances that would remove her daughter from her accustomed surroundings. It was one thing for a respectable Boston girl to sing in an opera—in a theater—among her own kind of high-minded men and women, and even in Boston itself Mary Eliza had not felt quite sure that Charlotte was not damaging her good name by participating in such a performance.

But in New Orleans! Notoriously a magnet for loose women and the sort of men who were not ashamed to seek such low society, New Orleans with its sinful aura thoroughly alarmed Charlotte's mother. If decent people might live there, she knew they probably were in some way infected by the Catholic religion of the majority: considering herself a liberal Unitarian, Mary Eliza still shuddered at the pernicious influence of the Roman faith. Furthermore, the climate at the extreme south on the Mississippi River was certainly most unhealthful, with its moist heat fostering the spread of horrible disease, despite the city's growing importance as a trading center.

Altogether, Mary Eliza detested the idea of Charlotte's going to New Orleans. Why could she not sensibly stay in Boston? But Charlotte would not heed her mother's warnings, and her mother could not afford to pick up dear Susan and the two boys to go along and protect her willful elder daughter.

Thus, with just Mr. and Mrs. Wood to guard her, soon after her nineteenth birthday Charlotte stubbornly embarked for New Orleans aboard a coastal sailing ship whose name the young singer considered wonderfully appropriate. It was the *Star*.

Down to New Orleans

A NOTHER sort of omen greeted Charlotte upon the *Star*'s arrival at the foreign-seeming city on the lower Mississippi. There the rainy season had lasted longer than usual, delaying the construction of the grand new St. Charles Theatre, where the opera company was scheduled as the first attraction. So this most elegant playhouse on the North American continent, capable of seating *four thousand* people, would be only barely ready by their opening date.

Yet the smell of damp plaster distressed Charlotte less during their rehearsals than the vast expanse she faced from the stage. Reaching skyward, four tiers of richly curtained box seats overlooked the enormous main gallery. Yet no amount of crimson velvet or carved mahogany dissipated the peculiar chill in the air as she valiantly practiced, nor did the thought that the audience here would have an exceptional familiarity with fine music warm her.

For New Orleans, in the 1830s, was probably the most sophisticated city in the United States. Its unique history of alternating French and Spanish domination had left it with more of a European taste, musically as well as in the consuming of splendid meals, than any of the rest of the young America. Also, as Mary Eliza had feared, its varied entertainments along with its ideal trading location made it a magnet every winter for tens of thousands of men bent on enjoying every sort of pleasure. Had Charlotte been beautiful, undoubtedly her debut there would have been welcomed, no matter how she sang.

But on December 1, 1835, when this earnest, square-faced young woman from Boston stood on the St. Charles stage, pretending to be the Countess Almaviva, the worldly New Orleans gaped in silence. Though her singing was inaudible to start with, then shrill, and then inaudible again, nobody even bothered to boo her. Of course, applause was out of the question. And the critics in the next day's newspapers mostly just ignored her, only one of them taking the trouble to remark of Miss Cushman that she "made the worst countess we have had the honor of seeing for some time."

The full extent of the disaster did not become clear, though, until several weeks had elapsed. Gamely Charlotte tried to seem unhurt. Despite the turmoil of emotion churning within her, she kept right on rehearsing—and performing—going back and forth from the theater to her garret room in a nearby boardinghouse, hardly noticing the colorful street crowds or the quaintly French architecture of the buildings she passed. If sheer determination could achieve victory after such a defeat, she would show this heartless city! At first Mr. Wood and his wife encouraged her just as they had been doing ever since she had come to sing for them at their Boston hotel suite. Then Charlotte sensed a change in their manner, while she also realized something appalling herself.

She had lost her voice. Oh, she could still produce low tones of some purity, but her shrillness when she sang any of the higher notes in the arias she had easily trilled a few months earlier made the conclusion inescapable. While such vocal collapses were not unheard of, why— why had it happened to her?

Maybe the sudden strain of attempting to project her voice toward the topmost boxes of this huge theater had been the cause. Or possibly the sticky, humid climate of New Orleans, and all that damp plaster. Most likely, however, the main reason was that, at nineteen, and without sufficient training, she had been pushed beyond prudence to sing too much, too soon. Was this the fault of the Woods and the coach they had provided for her? Having so much broader a musical background than she did, should they not have known better? Or had they been taking advantage of her inexperience to profit themselves by sponsoring a new attraction?

If questions like these agitated Charlotte, she gave no sign of it. Indeed, there was so much else to worry her that she could not waste energy blaming the Woods—nor did they abandon her. She had a six-month contract with them, and they assigned her increasingly less taxing roles requiring a minimum of singing, or no singing at all, while she painfully considered what to do next.

How could she slink home to Boston and confess herself a failure? Wouldn't her mother crow then! So week after week, as Charlotte continued sending most of her earnings to Mary Eliza and the children, she brooded over a desperate step because she could see no other solution, and finally she went to see the owner of the St. Charles Theatre. He told her what she had hoped—and dreaded. "You ought to be an actress," he said.

In these miserable months she had learned to walk like a countess, if not sing acceptably, and her speaking voice remained rich and deep. On stage, confronting thousands of eyes beyond the footlights, Charlotte felt stupendously alive. By saucily adjusting the fringe of her shawl, she could make a wave of laughter sweep the immense theater; it was a form of power she *knew* she could master. Also, it was a way even a young woman could hope to earn more money than most men.

And yet Charlotte knew, too, that her mother would be horrified at having a daughter become an actress. The old idea that females who exhibited themselves in public this way were surely immoral had by no means been forgotten in Boston; even Charlotte, with her strong convictions about self-reliance, was concerned over whether she could avoid the debasing influence of a stage career. Opera, somehow, had a higher standing, but now opera was beyond her. Grimly she concluded that she had no choice except to seek help from the actor to whom the theater owner referred her.

It happened, incredibly, that this established performer named James Barton was planning to follow the opera troupe's run at the new theater with a production of Shakespeare's *Macbeth,* and he had yet to find a woman he deemed acceptable in the crucial role of the bloodthirsty Lady Macbeth. Beauty was not required for this pivotal character; raw power was. That Barton instantly saw the possibilities of a novice still only nineteen, who had never appeared in any dramatic presentation, is an unmatchable defense of the trite phrase that truth is stranger than any fiction.

Even so, Barton had moments of distrust. Rehearsing with Charlotte in her garret, he became irritated and then infuriated by her vexing refusal to let herself express emotion to the full capacity he had perceived. Late one evening, when she was almost woodenly repeating Shakespeare's passionate poetry, Barton lost his temper and shouted at her.

What made her think she had the makings of a real actress? If he had briefly believed this, now he knew his mistake. She no more possessed the talent to portray Lady Macbeth than an oyster did. She was impossible! She was bound to fail! Let her go back to Boston and make her living by taking in laundry!

Then Charlotte turned on Barton like a female panther and furiously charged him with crimes they both knew he was innocent of, but in the process she showed the power she had hitherto been afraid to unleash because she was torn by her feeling that to do so would be unladylike. In the midst of her tirade, she and Barton both suddenly broke down laughing almost hysterically. Whether he had purposely

Charlotte Cushman as Lady Macbeth.

taught her a lesson, as he later would claim, or whether he had simply exploded with frustration, they both understood that he had achieved something extraordinary. He had turned a respectable young woman from Boston into America's first convincing Lady Macbeth.

After that, Charlotte's performance in Shakespeare's tragedy on the stage of the St. Charles seemed almost an anticlimax, at least to her. Now she was positive she could make her fortune—and save her family—by acting professionally. When the New Orleans critics proceeded to herald her as the most promising dramatic actress America had yet produced, she could have remained there reaping the first rewards of success. But she longed to see her family, and she shrewdly preferred making her name famous beyond the isolated New Orleans—in New York.

If her story were fiction, Charlotte might be expected to follow her Southern triumph with an easy leap to stardom immediately on returning North. In fact, she did grandly send a note to the manager of New York's leading theater when she arrived there, letting him know that her services were available. And he rebuffed her presumption. If she would come and try out for a part, he might use her in minor roles. But that was only the beginning of her real-life struggle to find her way personally as well as professionally.

The process started with a three-year contract as a "walking lady"— which meant she would walk on stage night after night, playing every sort of supporting part from gypsy fortune-teller to Juliet's nursemaid. Though it was a rundown theater on the edge of a New York slum that hired her, still her pay of twenty dollars a week let her fulfill one goal. Charlotte wrote to her mother in Boston, insisting that she close the boardinghouse and bring the family to New York to make a home for her.

Mary Eliza was not sorry to receive this summons. If Charlotte could not be dissuaded from her disreputable course, at least a mother's influence might keep her from sinking into absolute disgrace. And as far as she herself was concerned, Mary Eliza could only welcome ending her drudgery on behalf of strangers in favor of the far less arduous task of keeping house for her own children or, rather, for three of them. Of course, eleven-year-old Gus would come with her; there must be a decent school he could attend in New York. Eighteen-year-old Charlie, clerking at a Boston store, could surely find a similar job in the bigger city.

But her darling Susan, fourteen in this summer of 1836 and as gracefully willowy a young lady as there ever was—Susan must not be exposed to the roughness of New York, let alone the tainted atmosphere of theatrical immorality surrounding Charlotte. So Mary Eliza racked her brain for a suitable guardian to protect Susan, and came up with a candidate who proved willing. Elkanah Cushman, frail and ailing, was still living with his married daughter, Isabella, and Isabella agreed to harbor her young stepsister.

How did Susan herself like this idea? It is hard to be sure because only a minimum of evidence about her life would be preserved. She left no memoirs, and just a few letters, so we shall frequently have to wonder what she thought and, indeed, whether she really was so blandly sweet and pretty as most people assumed her to be. But in Boston, under Isabella's protection, she soon became the main character in a most bizarre melodrama: it makes her interesting, and it also affected her older sister indelibly. Before going into this fantastic episode, though, it is necessary to follow the rest of her family to New York—and Albany.

For Charlotte's three-year contract, literally, went up in smoke. Not only did that rundown theater burn to the ground, leaving her penniless instead of in a position to support her mother and brothers, but her supply of costumes that she had borrowed a hundred and fifty dollars to buy—in those days, actresses had to provide their own stage wardrobe—also was destroyed. In debt, she was obliged to take the first job she could find. It required sailing more than a hundred miles north on the Hudson River to New York's old Dutch state capital. Of necessity, Charlotte's mother and two brothers made the trek with her.

Professionally, the move had its advantages. Again as walking lady,

Charlotte played a large variety of roles, gaining invaluable experience. Also, she found quite an unexpectedly lively society among the state officials at the hotel where the Cushmans resided, and she discovered the pleasure of being the center of attraction while witty gentlemen vied to trade quips with her. One of these almost succeeded in convincing her that he might make a fitting husband, though she escaped, as she would later say, sighing deeply. Still only twenty, she had already decided that no woman who had an artistic gift could marry and be a good wife: of her own gift, she held not the slightest question.

Yet Albany would always remain in her memory as the scene of her worst personal suffering. Her cherished brother Gus had his twelfth birthday while they were there, and she offered him anything in the world he wanted as his present. When he chose a spirited horse, so that he could ride back and forth on weekends from his boarding school, she was delighted. Charlotte herself, in sleek black riding habit, loved nothing better than a bracing gallop out in the countryside. But Gus, for all his manly vigor, found one terrible afternoon that he could not control his mount. The horse reared, and the boy tumbled head first onto the frozen ground. By the time a farmer who had witnessed the accident reached the huddled body of the young rider, Gus was dead.

To Charlotte, the death of her beloved brother was a blow even time would not soften. She took the jacket he had been wearing that fatal afternoon, and wrapped it carefully to keep with her always. Deeply religious in her own private way, she tortured herself with a thought of starkly Puritan origin. Perhaps her mother was right in claiming there was something basically sinful about theatrical performing. Could it be that God had punished her by taking away Augustus? Even the fire last autumn in New York could have been a warning. In this overwrought state Charlotte also had to worry about Susan.

While Isabella in no way mistreated the child, her notions about Susan's best interests were, at the very least, unsettling. The difficulty revolved around an elderly friend of Elkanah's, a man with no close relatives of his own and quite impressive prosperity. This Mr. Merriman had advanced a startling idea. Why could he not legally adopt Susan? Her youthful charm had so endeared her to him that he wanted to provide for her education and future, but his doing so might antagonize some of his distant connections to the extent that they would thwart his will—unless, by law, Susan was entitled to his money.

Isabella thought the idea not only plausible but generous. Mary Eliza could not agree. To give up her favorite was impossible, and she made this clear to Isabella. But a few months later even more disquieting word came from Boston.

Mr. Merriman was rapidly declining, and to soothe his final weeks on earth he had asked that Susan visit him and ease his pain by reading aloud to him. Because she had such a gentle voice, besides being a fine reader, Isabella saw no harm in allowing the child thus to console their father's friend. Indeed, Isabella further communicated an offer she considered highly advantageous to her young stepsister.

Old Mr. Merriman, on the verge of dying, desired nothing more than to assure Susan's right to his money. Now it was too late to go through the formalities of adoption, but not too late for a simpler legal ceremony. In short, he wished to marry Susan so that, as his widow, she would unquestionably inherit his savings. And Isabella herself strongly recommended the step.

Reading Isabella's letter, both Charlotte and her mother were initially horrified. Susan was only fourteen and Mr. Merriman nearly seventy. How could Isabella advise such an extraordinary match? And what did Susan herself think of it? Surely, the hope of a monetary gain could not justify such impropriety! And yet, to have the child forever secure from financial want . . . It was a temptation Mary Eliza could not reject without seeing firsthand how matters stood. So she hurried to Boston.

There she let herself be swayed more by Isabella's positive enthusiasm than by Susan's piteous weeping. Well, of course, the child could not grasp the prudence of a mere formality. To Mary Eliza's endless shame, she virtually forced her fourteen-year-old daughter to go through a deathbed marriage ceremony.

But Mr. Merriman did not expire. Instead, in the next several months he miraculously regained health until a letter from Susan conveyed staggering news. She was pregnant! And Mr. Merriman, no doubt aware of what the reaction of Susan's mother must be, had stolen off, leaving his young wife all on her own.

At least that was a mercy. Under the law at that time, any wife lacked grounds for legally separating from her husband—unless *he* deserted *her*. So Susan owed no further duty to Mr. Merriman and, at fifteen, she desperately needed help. Her mother, torn by her guilt about her own part in this sordid affair, wrung her hands and wept at the ruin of her beautiful daughter's life. No matter that Susan had been seduced after a proper wedding; the disgrace was almost as bad as if she were about to become an unwed mother. People would think the worst anyway because Susan looked so young, Mary Eliza wailed. So it was up to Charlotte to take charge in this crisis, and she briskly arranged for Susan to join them.

By now the family was back in New York City. Charlotte had approached the manager of the famed Park Theatre more humbly after her seven months in Albany, and a trial run had proved her ability. Thus she had a three-year contract as a member of an outstanding company, which signified a major advance in her career. Not that she was treated as a star or even received leading roles; such status was reserved for a handful of performers, most of them from England, whose international reputation enabled them to travel about, taking top billing, and being paid accordingly, wherever they went. Still, Charlotte's twenty dollars a week, supplemented by her brother's wages of about half that amount for working in a store, enabled the Cushmans to live quite comfortably in a rented house not far from the theater.

Here Susan gave birth to her baby on March 4, 1838, two weeks before she herself turned sixteen. The infant was a husky boy she

named Edwin, but his Aunt Charlotte promptly dubbed him "Bub."
Surrounded as he was by female relatives who could not resist spoiling
him, Bub quickly learned that Auntie would always bring him sweet-
meats even when his mother and grandmother tried to be severe with
him. For all practical purposes, Auntie was undoubtedly the head of
the household.

So it was she who solved the problem of what Susan could do with
herself beyond watching Bub, which his grandmother was more than
willing to take over. At sixteen, Susan was just emerging from her
own childhood, and surely it was a mistake to suppose that her unfortunate marriage had ended her every chance of enjoying the rest
of her life. As a start, Charlotte suggested that Susan might help her
a good deal by holding the script of a new play and reading out cues
while her big sister was memorizing her own part. Then when Susan
proved wonderfully adept in her prompting, Charlotte decided she
would make an actress out of Susan, too!

Poor Mary Eliza could only shake her head mournfully while Charlotte coached her dear, fallen daughter. But during the next year
Susan surprised Charlotte by the eagerness with which she applied
herself to practicing little scenes. If Charlotte had imagined that Susan,
for all of her gentle manner, might yearn to stand in the center of a
stage and be applauded even more thunderously than her overpower-
ing older sister, perhaps there would have been less surprise. Charlotte,
though, could not conceive of Susan as a rival; she merely thought
that Susan, with her fragile beauty, might do quite well playing the
sort of girlish heroine sturdy Charlotte could never attempt. Instead
of competing with each other, they would complement each other—
presenting an uncommon attraction bound to arouse much curiosity
among theatergoers.

The Park's manager seemed to agree when he hired Susan for twelve
dollars a week. Then, in the spring of 1839, she began appearing with
Charlotte in a variety of dramas, most destined to be forgotten. Befitting Susan's lesser experience and salary, the posters announcing
their performances described them as: MISS CUSHMAN and Her Sister.

If the slight provoked Susan, Charlotte also suffered because the critics universally emphasized how pretty Susan was, adding insult to injury by bemoaning Miss Cushman's own lack of feminine charm. Still, both sisters won increasing praise for their artistry, and increasingly, they were assigned to play together in important dramas. In Shakespeare's *Hamlet,* for instance, Susan won sympathy as the melancholy hero's doomed love, Ophelia, while Charlotte made the rafters resound with her passion in the role of Hamlet's evil mother, Queen Gertrude.

Although sisterly rivalry certainly did begin seething beneath the surface, Charlotte and Susan were united on one point: they were underpaid. Actually, however, they earned much more than was usual in their era, when women were not expected to work outside their homes and the comparatively few who did so received pitifully low wages. Yet the income of the Cushman sisters was puny in comparison

Susan Cushman in her early twenties.

with the huge fees that rewarded visiting English stars. So Charlotte hatched a plan. After her contract expired, and no better terms were offered, she and Susan, too, left the Park Theatre's renowned company. Boldly, Charlotte undertook the management of a company of her own—in Philadelphia.

It was a brave experiment for a female—and, more than a century later, we can scarcely imagine Charlotte's tribulations. By venturing to direct men, she marked herself as unwomanly. Furthermore, just because she was an actress it was assumed that she lacked a lady's unsoiled purity. Despite her entirely respectable behavior offstage, Philadelphia by and large exceeded even her mother in severity. At church one Sunday morning a gentleman arose and objected loudly when he became aware of the identity of the young woman in the adjoining pew. Persons employed upon the stage polluted the atmosphere of a religious service, he asserted, then walked out with his family. But intolerance like this was the least of Charlotte's problems, and she soon found broader-minded friends.

Professionally, though, she could not cope with her new problems as easily. Though she and Susan again demonstrated their appeal to audiences and won much critical approval, the business details involved in operating a theater exasperated Charlotte. Also, depressed economic conditions made the venture less successful financially than it might have been in good times. Above all, the difficulties of being in charge of stagehands, instead of being able to concentrate on her acting, besides the frictions of living and working with a younger sister who more and more appeared to forget how she had ever gotten behind the footlights, made Charlotte finally decide that her own career must come first.

Now Susan was launched. Let her try making her way by herself, at least temporarily. If Charlotte was ever to reach *her* potential, artistically as well as financially, there was only one way to do it. She must go to London.

For even though the American Revolution back in 1776 had ended this country's colonial status, Britain still preserved its superiority as far as the arts were concerned. Before any actor or actress could attain the standing of a star—and command a star's reward of tens of thousands of dollars a year—it was necessary to win the approval of English critics. So Charlotte, after three ever more tense years in Philadelphia, resolved to test herself by trying to conquer the British capital.

In the late summer of 1844, when she was twenty-eight, Charlotte borrowed money for her passage overseas. While she was gone, Mary Eliza would continue caring for Bub, and Susan would earn what she could. Brother Charlie amiably accepted the plan; he never would stir any ripples.

Mainly because Charlotte realized that she might feel lost all by herself on the other side of the world, she did something a little startling before she sailed. She hired a personal maid. With her limited resources, she chose the fourteen-year-old daughter of a free black woman of good reputation. Young Sallie Mercer, a merry girl who needed only an opportunity to show an amazing range of talents, accompanied her from Philadelphia to New York, where they boarded their ship.

On October 26, 1844, Sallie and her new employer stood on deck watching the island of Manhattan recede into a pale blue haze. The vessel on which they were daring the ocean had been named after one of the most famous of English actors; it was the *Garrick*. What a hopeful omen, Charlotte thought.

Conquest in London

THE voyage was rough, but Charlotte reached the huge, exciting city of London in high spirits. From her eight years of theatrical experience, she already knew some of the luminaries of the British stage, and she intended to meet a good many others. In her luggage she carried no less than eighty letters of introduction.

She even found a few inquiries from managers awaiting her at her hotel, but she was in no hurry to arrange her British debut. At this point in her career she would not settle for merely assisting an established star. No, she must capture the full attention of London's influential theater critics with a spectacular display of her own. Otherwise, she might be brushed off as just a capable nonentity—and her trip would be wasted.

Since the kind of offer Charlotte wanted was not immediately forthcoming, she bided her time. With Sallie, she went off to visit several shipboard acquaintances around the British countryside. She also spent a few weeks in France, taking a close look at the acting technique of the famous theater companies of Paris, which fascinated her despite her inability to understand a single word of their language.

Then, with her money nearly exhausted, she and Sallie were reduced to humble lodgings on their return to London. In later years Sallie would brag a little about her skill at economizing. "I always bought the baker's dozen of muffins for the sake of the extra one," she said, "and we ate them all, no matter how stale they were." Day after day they existed on just a single mutton chop apiece, plus those stale muffins. Still Charlotte would not compromise—nor did she starve.

Early one morning, too early for a polite visit, Sallie looked out a window and spied a man nervously pacing the sidewalk outside their door. Charlotte was thrilled to recognize the manager of the Princess Theatre. "He is anxious," Charlotte told Sallie. "I can make my own terms." And she did. For it not only happened that he badly needed a new attraction to bolster his box-office receipts, but like James Barton back in New Orleans, he had somehow sensed a magnetic force in this tall, blunt, almost homely American woman.

Thus for Charlotte's first appearance on a London stage, he agreed to let her choose whatever role she wished from his company's repertoire. Thereafter, it was further arranged, she would have some choice about the parts she performed in the series of plays that had already been announced, though she would also be expected to oblige him by supporting other members of his company quite often.

On the matter of money, he was not overly generous. He would pay her seven pounds a night, about thirty-five dollars then, which satisfied her despite its being just a fraction of what the company's male lead would receive. As her closest friend, Emma Stebbins, would explain many years afterward: "It was not money she sought, but *recognition*."

To dazzle the London critics on her opening night, Charlotte picked a tragic opus that has long since been forgotten. Entitled *Fazio,* its plot, in the 1980s, may seem ridiculous: a medieval scholar named Fazio, failing in his efforts to create gold by combining various powders, steals a miser's hoard, claiming to have produced it by one of his experiments. Suddenly rich, he abandons his wife for a temptress. Then the jealous wife informs the authorities of Fazio's theft, assuming her husband will merely be reprimanded if he returns the money, but the husband is condemned to hang. The wife, in a frenzy of remorse, begs clemency for him. Not succeeding, she turbulently dies herself of a broken heart as the curtain finally descends.

Yet Charlotte could not have made a sounder selection, given the 1840s taste for explosively emotional theatrical display. Portraying the wife, Bianca, she only slowly and gradually showed her power. But after Bianca's discovery of her husband's treachery, her opportunities for dominating the stage were unmatched in all of Shakespeare's superior drama. During the last act she rose to a magnificent surge of agitated pathos as she collapsed and died. So her first London audience, on the night of February 14, 1845, was totally enraptured.

"Bravo! Bravo!" The shouting surpassed any acclaim she had ever received in New York. People stood on their seats, clapping wildly and waving handkerchiefs. From the wings Sallie grinned and hollered, "You've got 'em, missus, you've got 'em!" Sallie was right.

The next day's London papers celebrated a great event in the annals of the British stage. "America has long owed us a heavy dramatic debt for enticing away from us so many of our best actors," said the *Sun*. "She has now more than repaid it by giving us the greatest of actresses, Miss Cushman." Of Charlotte herself, the *Herald* told its readers, "Miss Cushman is tall and commanding, having a fine stage figure." The *Times* extolled her earnestness, her intensity, her ability to dart rapidly from emotion to emotion. In all, even Charlotte was satisfied by the scope of her conquest.

And yet there was one person's approval she craved most of all. Maybe now, at last, her mother would value her as much as Susan, so Charlotte immediately sent off a packet of press clippings to Philadelphia, along with a letter saying these would tell "in so much better language than I could of my brilliant and triumphant success in London." Still, Charlotte repeatedly dwelled on the subject during the next several weeks.

". . . it is far, far beyond my most *sanguine expectations,*" she wrote home on March 2. "Why should I hesitate (unless through a fear that I might seem egotistical) to tell you all my triumphs, all my success?"

Then toward the end of the month she made it clear that socially as well as artistically she had moved into a different sphere:

> I have been so crowded with company since I have acted. . . . Invitations pour in for every night that I do not act, and all the day I have a steady stream of callers so that I am never without less than six people in the room; and I am so tired when it comes time for me to go to the theatre that Sallie has to hold my cup of tea for me to drink it.
>
> It seems almost exaggerated, this account; but indeed you would laugh if you could see the way I am besieged, and if you could see the heaps of complimentary letters and notes you would be amused. All this, as you may imagine, reconciles me more to England, and now I think I might be willing to stay longer. If my family were only with me, I think I could be content.

Originally, Charlotte had thought she might stay abroad only six or seven months, just until she could accumulate a scrapbook of praise from London critics that would insure her future stardom in Philadelphia, New York, and Boston. Yet the degree of success she had achieved overnight clearly was changing her mind. Instead of just a month or two in London, the manager of the Princess Theatre had begun predicting an unprecedented run throughout the spring, even stretching into summer. Besides playing Bianca once or twice a week, Charlotte was to alternate as Lady Macbeth and also—to prove her versatility—as the spirited Rosaline in Shakespeare's comedy *Love's Labour's Lost*.

Furthermore, theater managers in Edinburgh, Dublin, and practically every other city all over the British Isles were begging her to appear with their companies and offering fees too handsome to be disregarded. So Charlotte soon came to a momentous decision based on much soul-searching.

What had, in the first place, drawn her to strive for a stage career? Surely her goal had always been to earn enough to support her family in respectable style. Well, now she had within her grasp an opportunity to guarantee the future welfare of her mother, of Susan and little Bub, and of her feckless brother Charlie. If she stayed five years in England, Charlotte calculated, she could accumulate a small fortune, beyond all necessary expenses, of at least fifty thousand dollars. Prudently invested, this would protect them all forever as they placidly lived out the rest of their lives in some tidy cottage together, perhaps in a suburb of Boston. Wouldn't such a peaceful retirement among proper New Englanders make even her mother forget the turmoil of their earlier years?

Certain herself of the soundness of her plan, Charlotte immediately set it in motion. Her first step was to summon her family from Philadelphia, for how could they be separated five whole years? By the end of May she had saved enough to send them money to pay their passage overseas. Anticipating their arrival in mid-July, she searched the residential quarters of London, seeking a furnished house that would suit them all. For her mother's sake, she wanted a pleasant garden where birds might divert her: Mary Eliza loved watching birds flit among trees and flowers. But the garden must also contain space enough for seven-year-old Bub to play ball. And since Charlotte herself had been making so many new friends, the house should be sufficiently roomy for gracious entertaining. By the beginning of July she had settled on an attractive residence in the Bayswater neighborhood, close to the theater district.

Yet none of Charlotte's arranging considered what Susan might prefer. For Susan had always leaned on her mother or Charlotte: she had never seemed capable of taking any initiative herself. Charlotte had never gathered so much as a hint that Susan had any strong opinions of her own.

In the first joy of their family reunion, amid happy tears and hugging, no unexpected assertiveness marred their pleasure. Only Charlotte's nephew expressed some dissatisfaction. Tall for his age and accustomed to be heeded, he let Auntie understand that he would no longer answer to a silly nickname. But calling him Edwin would be no improvement, she suggested. Agreeing with her, he settled on Ned.

In only a matter of weeks, however, Charlotte noticed a new assurance on Susan's part. After her elder sister's departure from Philadelphia, Susan herself had kept on playing Ophelia, or the lovely Desdemona in *Othello,* and the placards outside the theaters where she performed gave her the satisfaction of identifying her fully, as Miss Susan Cushman. Since she had dissolved the last vestige of her hateful tie to Mr. Merriman by securing a divorce, that *was* her name again.

Susan's evidence of maturity pleased Charlotte. Certainly it was time—Susan had turned twenty-three on her last birthday—that she ceased behaving as their mother's baby. What did increasingly irritate Charlotte, however, was one sign after another that Susan and Mary Eliza had formed a sort of alliance against her. They showed this by their treatment of some of Charlotte's new friends.

The week after her family's arrival in London, Charlotte marked her twenty-ninth birthday, feeling blessed by having them all with her. Still, she had spent the preceding nine months on her own, achieving fame and attracting a multitude of stimulating acquaintances. Among those who most fascinated her were several so-called new women, making careers for themselves as writers, and they saw her triumph as an inspiration for talented women everywhere. One of these, a poet who chose to wear mannish clothing, had become Charlotte's particular friend. Eliza Cook appreciated Charlotte's individuality, and she understood the personal sacrifice involved when a woman of deep emotional capacity gave up marriage in favor of artistic fulfillment.

But Charlotte's mother and sister united in their rudeness to Eliza Cook or any other unconventional visitor at the Bayswater house. After just a few months Charlotte found herself recalling how confined she had felt in Philadelphia by her mother's disapproval of a similar friendship with the daughter of a noted painter. She also found herself seething at the prospect of being hemmed in like a child by parental, and even sisterly, restrictions throughout her life. How could she stand such meddling?

Despite this sort of underlying tension, though, Charlotte and Susan remained on good terms outwardly. Just as in America, now in London the elder sister brought the younger forward—and within a few months they were appearing together in theaters all over Britain. Most spectacularly, they played the ill-fated young lovers of Shakespeare's *Romeo and Juliet.*

It was not unheard of for a female to attempt the role of Romeo. Theatrical tradition held that no actor could achieve the professional polish required for speaking Romeo's lines with sufficient fervor until he looked too old for the part. So Charlotte was far from the first experienced actress who thought she could do better at it than most men. Even so, the Cushman sisters created a storm of interest, accompanied by a strong undercurrent of malicious whispering, as they toured Scotland, Ireland, and practically every province of England in their production of the famous tragedy.

The mere fact that Charlotte and Susan were sisters stirred much of the talk, which led to full houses wherever they went. Nor did the audiences feel cheated, for Susan's sweet Juliet won plaudits almost as enthusiastic as the praise showered on Charlotte's vigorous Romeo. Beneath all the public acclaim, though, unpleasant rumors about both sisters were widely spread.

While Britain tended to make less of an issue about personal immorality among theatrical performers than was the case in America, these American sisters had been publicized as highly respectable young women. But were they? Inevitably, gossip arose about Susan when it became known that the younger *Miss* Cushman had brought a child

A contemporary artist's etching of the Cushman sisters as
Romeo and Juliet.

of hers to England with her. To counter various nasty inferences before they started showing up in print, Charlotte insisted on proving Susan had been married at the time of her son's birth by circulating copies of her sister's marriage and divorce certificates.

The innuendos about Charlotte herself were harder to counteract. In those days the subject of homosexuality could not even be mentioned in public, and it was assumed that reputable women never so much as suspected there could be a physical relationship between two persons of the same sex. Still, there was a prevailing prejudice against women whose behavior might be considered mannish; undoubtedly, that vague prejudice explained the attitude of Susan and her mother toward some of Charlotte's friends. Otherwise Charlotte's association with these friends caused hardly any attention in tolerant London, but in the provinces her own unfeminine garb and masculine gusto in the role of Romeo led to murmurings regarding an unspeakable tendency.

It was a whispering campaign Charlotte could not silence, but she traced it to its source. Actors were notoriously jealous of one another, and she proved, at least to her own satisfaction, that a Macbeth whom she had deprived of applause by her overwhelming performances as Lady Macbeth was the originator of these rumors. But theatrical jealousy could spread its poison even within the same family.

By the summer of 1846, a year after Susan's arrival in England, Charlotte could not avoid noticing her sister's envy of her own higher standing and higher pay. Quibbles about the way their posters emphasized the elder Miss Cushman were only a symptom of the younger Miss Cushman's discontent. To Charlotte, the idea that Susan deserved equal billing was absurd, and yet it was not merely Susan who obviously felt this way; their mother did, too. Even one of Charlotte's literary acquaintances, visiting Bayswater, noticed Mrs. Cushman's resentment of her elder daughter's greater fame. To her own diary this visitor confided, "The younger daughter Susan was the mother's favorite."

Had Susan expressed her antagonism merely to Charlotte, they might have fought openly and cleared the air. Instead, in the autumn of 1846 Susan wrote a letter that set off a private demonstration of the elder Miss Cushman's capacity for behind-the-scenes plotting. Susan addressed her letter to none other than the disgruntled Macbeth—a flamboyant actor named William Macready—and Susan asked him to consider hiring her as a member of his company.

Of course, Charlotte swiftly learned about the letter. To remain a star, it was essential to develop a private network of informants as a means of self-protection. Precisely how Charlotte managed to make Mr. Macready become aware that he would be sorry if he employed Miss Susan Cushman we cannot say. All we can be sure of is an entry in Macready's diary noting that he had endeavored "to persuade [Susan] of the mutual folly of herself and sister separating, but urging her to conciliate and succumb rather than part."

After this trial balloon of Susan's burst, it should have been clear to both sisters that, sooner or later, they must go their own ways. Yet how could they do so without inflicting terrible pain on their mother? Even Charlotte, chafing at Mary Eliza's complaints and unfairness, could not bring herself simply to move and leave the others to manage on their own in Bayswater. As for Susan, she had to worry not only about her own future but also Ned's.

Her son, whether or not she ever put the thought plainly to herself, presented a major obstacle along her most logical path toward freedom from Charlotte's domineering. For Susan, with her delicate beauty, had no difficulty in attracting male admirers. Yet most men in her day would not be willing to marry a young woman subject to embarrassing questions about her past, besides being encumbered by a child of questionable parentage. At least, the kind of prosperous, well-regarded man Susan considered as a possible husband would be put off by her special disadvantages.

Thus the uneasy acting partnership between the two sisters continued another year and a half. Professionally, they continued to reap glowing reviews and appealing monetary awards. But personally, they were not happy. Charlotte could not help lording it over Susan at every opportunity, and Susan could no longer disguise her hostility toward her overbearing sister.

In Liverpool the friction between them almost caused a break. Susan's restlessness led her into a flirtation with a young actor possessing a remarkable mustache, who also happened to be married. Susan, no less than Charlotte, regarded unwed love affairs as disgraceful, but when her sister took to lecturing her about the danger of this connection, it was more than Susan could bear. In Liverpool a rich and unmarried son of a family making a fortune by manufacturing industrial chemicals also was courting Miss Susan Cushman. Whether or not his pursuit would have succeeded if she had been more calm we do not know.

As it was, when Mr. James Sheridan Muspratt sent his card repeatedly to the stage door, the younger Miss Cushman deigned to welcome him. Would she have supper with him? Why not! And visit his family's estate, Seaforth Hall? Of course!

Indeed, Seaforth Hall, as its name indicated, faced onto an exhilarating prospect of open water looking toward Ireland. The grime and squalor of industrial Liverpool behind it could not even be suspected amid the gardens and the splendor of the Muspratt mansion. Nor was young Mr. Muspratt lacking culture. Among his greatest friends was the novelist Charles Dickens. So Susan decided that this young man might serve her purpose.

At an elaborate New Year's ball that Charlotte also attended, the engagement of the heir to the Muspratt fortune and his beautiful replica of Shakespeare's Juliet was formally announced. There remained only a short schedule of theatrical engagements that the prospective bride was bound to fulfill. Then, on March 22, 1848, less than a week after her twenty-sixth birthday, Susan solemnly said, "I do," and became Mrs. James Sheridan Muspratt.

New Ties

S USAN, of course, retired from the stage, removing the surface cause of the friction between her and Charlotte. Their rivalry did not end, though; it merely operated in a different way. Actually, the ceremony that turned a pretty actress into a pampered wife, proudly reigning at an elegant new mansion called Rose Hill Hall, had many repercussions in the Cushman family.

Charlotte was approaching the age of thirty-two when Susan ceased competing with her theatrically. By her own choice, because she had always felt that her career must come first, Charlotte had years ago given up any thought of marriage herself. Square-jawed or not, she had had her chances, and doubtless she still could snare a husband if she was willing to vow obedience. But that was impossible!

And yet how could she have been so childish as to assume that merely remaining single would guarantee her personal freedom? After seeing Susan's awesome house, presided over by a haughty butler with a staff of maids and footmen, Charlotte realized that she could no longer endure the restrictions of Bayswater. Whatever her mother said, it was high time to move out—and live as *she* wished.

Certainly she would continue to supplement dull Brother Charlie's trifling wages as a clerk in an insurance office, so that he and their mother would suffer no privation. As it happened, however, they declined her offer. They assured her that they would rather find themselves a modest row house near his work, Mary Eliza tearfully adding that she might feel happier making a home for her son in a more humble neighborhood, reminding her of her old part of Boston. So be it, Charlotte would visit them when she could.

But for herself she leased a fine house opposite one of London's most fashionable parks. Installing a butler of her own to supervise a cook and housemaid—with Sallie, naturally, continuing as her invaluable personal aide, at home and at every theater where she performed—Charlotte prepared, finally, to enjoy her success. She held regular receptions at which the conversation sparkled like the rare wines she served her guests. In turn, she received more invitations to the city's most fascinating gatherings than she could possibly accept. What Charlotte had failed to anticipate, however, was the empty feeling all this left her with, once she had grown accustomed to the glitter.

Then her solution of a professional problem cured her loneliness, too. Hers was a period in theatrical history when the public associated every star with about a dozen roles and, while novelties were occasionally introduced, it was mainly the old favorites that audiences demanded. Lacking Susan's reliable support, Charlotte soon found that she could not depend on theater managers to do their own job properly. One horrible night she had to play opposite a drunken Juliet who nearly toppled off her balcony. So Charlotte began seeking some young hopeful whom she could train to appear with her in the plays that had become the staples of her every engagement.

Not long afterward a shy young woman hesitantly came to Charlotte's dressing room. Matilda Hays, despite her timidity, yearned to be an actress. Miss Cushman's electric performance had so stunned her that she thought—she hoped—was it even the least bit conceivable that *she* might be given lessons?

Charlotte glanced more carefully at Miss Hays, who was slender and had a pleasing if not pretty face. A few questions of her own established that Miss Hays was twenty-eight, without any family connections that would prevent her travel in any direction. Perceiving a certain charm about this totally inexperienced applicant, Charlotte impulsively agreed to coach her for the next several months. If Matilda proved teachable, here would be her new Juliet.

Matilda Hays did well enough to play a season with Charlotte, and even though her acting was hardly inspired, her devotion touched Charlotte deeply. Certainly Matilda would never dream of competing with her. Almost as if Charlotte had found a new sister, who would always look up to her and be grateful to her, soothing her personal loneliness the way a true sister should, the eminent Miss Cushman urged Matilda to share her life. For nearly ten years they would be inseparable.

These were mostly happy years, but hectic, too, at least at the outset. Despite Charlotte's reliance on Matilda, she by no means lost touch with Susan. They wrote to each other regularly, and Charlotte paid frequent short visits to rest and give advice. Then, eighteen months after Susan became Mrs. Muspratt, she welcomed her sister and her sister's tongue-tied friend for a longer, recuperative stay at Rose Hill Hall, outside Liverpool, prior to their embarking on a tremendous theatrical adventure.

They were bound for America, where Charlotte would—as she gleefully put it herself—"cash in" on her great English reputation. Engagements in every major city of the United States, from Boston to New Orleans, were being scheduled for her by a booking agent, at enormous fees. Perhaps she would even risk the rigors of the West, taking advantage of the golden opportunities beckoning her there. For she was prepared to work, work, work, during the next several years, so that she could leave the stage permanently well before she turned forty. Then, said Charlotte as she cast a meaningful gaze around Susan's elaborate garden, where they were sitting, she, too, would savor the rewards of wealth during the rest of her life.

We cannot say whether or not Susan Muspratt still envied her sister's fame, now that her own grandeur had obviously stimulated a new envy in Charlotte. As far as we know, her marriage was a happy one. Already she had a darling, if frail, little daughter, Ida, and two more girls would be born to her during the next few years. Though Liverpool could not bear comparison with London, in Liverpool Susan was a great lady now. Her sole source of distress seems to have been that her rich and handsome husband, despite his cultural interests, which softened his businessman's hardness, could not help objecting to his wife's way of spoiling her son, Ned.

By now Ned was past eleven and, to his mother, a boy of rare promise. In this, at least, Charlotte fully endorsed Susan's judgment. But Ned's stepfather decreed that the young man required disciplining, besides a proper education, which, to a well-off Englishman, signified an elite boarding school where privileged youths were subjected to icy baths and rigorous Latin as preparation for their future leadership.

Susan could not agree, nor could she fail to suffer when Ned took to sulking while her husband angrily reprimanded her son; it was a problem marring the tranquillity of her marriage. Yet Charlotte's warm sympathy with her sister on this matter opened a possibility that a few years later would demonstrate the positive aspect of the deep emotional ties linking these sisters. Meanwhile, Charlotte, accompanied by Matilda and Sallie, sailed back to America in August 1849.

She returned to find herself a heroine. "Hurray for our Charlotte!" people shouted when she landed in Boston. For the United States was still extremely sensitive to the opinions of European critics. On those rare occasions when foreign observers—especially the English, whose pre-1776 arrogance had not been forgotten—deigned to praise some American as rousingly as Charlotte Cushman had been praised, the nation's patriotic enthusiasm knew no bounds.

Yet the financial motive of Miss Cushman was not overlooked. The cover of a popular weekly emphasized this, under the headline: CUSHMANIA!, with a pair of cartoons displaying the change in her status—one captioned "Before," and the other "After." Before her London triumph an abject Charlotte begged an American theater manager to allow her on his stage. But after London the same manager on bended knee, holding up a large bag labeled $$, implored the regal star to sign on the dotted line.

Such publicity made most Americans smile. Why, the lady was smart to ask a good price now that she had vindicated American talent in snobby London. Wherever she went, Charlotte drew full houses ready to cheer her exuberantly, and the most eminent of her fellow citizens, male and female, joined in the chorus of approval. In Boston she was bidden to dine with the poets Lowell and Longfellow; also, an as-yet uncelebrated writer of stories named Louisa May Alcott confided to her diary: "Saw Charlotte Cushman and had a stage struck fit."

Charlotte vastly relished being the focus of so much attention—wouldn't her *Mayflower* forebears be proud of her now! Yet she retained a sense of humility that tempered her tendency to behave like a queen. Through a window of her Philadelphia hotel, she heard the cracked voice of an old woman singing on the street below and, glancing down, she saw the poor thing holding out a battered hat for money. Reaching into her purse, she handed Sallie a wad of dollars. "I never hear a woman sing like that," Charlotte murmured, "but that I think I might have been doing it myself."

In New York a much deeper compassion made her abruptly cancel the rest of her engagement when she received a letter from Susan reporting that little Ida was grievously ill. Though transatlantic travel was no light matter in 1850, Charlotte immediately booked passage for Liverpool and stayed three weeks comforting her sister until Ida recovered. Back she went then to resume acting—and "cashing in."

Yet the next two years did not lack trauma. Though Matilda's

106

loyalty was unfaltering, her limited ability as an actress could not survive the pressures of continuously performing several different plays every week. Flustered repeatedly, she and Charlotte at last faced a painful decision. Thenceforth, Matilda would serve as a sort of personal secretary, relieving overburdened Sallie. Together, these two tried with only partial success to prevent unnecessary aggravations from draining Charlotte's energy.

Eminent or not, Miss Cushman still had to wait for trains in drafty railroad depots and subsist on greasy stew at inferior hotels in many cities. Aching with fatigue, sometimes so hoarse she could not speak until a doctor sprayed her throat with a searing medicine, Charlotte grew increasingly impatient for retirement. As she began counting the months, and wondering just how she would occupy herself when she no longer had to keep up this fearful grind, an unhappy letter from Susan set her quick mind on an exciting new track.

Susan's misery, predictably, involved Ned, who was now fourteen. He and his stepfather still could not get along with each other—and what could Susan do to protect her cherished son from the severity of the husband she also loved? In a flash Charlotte perceived the perfect answer. She was rich, she soon would have plenty of time, and she had always felt a special empathy with Ned. Suppose she herself legally adopted him!

Despite the slowness of mail service back and forth across the ocean, Charlotte received a reply to her letter sooner than she had dared to hope. It was agreed! No matter that Susan could not quite disguise her own qualms over giving up her son; the boy himself was perfectly willing to let Auntie assume his care, and so was Susan's husband. With remarkable dispatch, Charlotte went through the formalities in New York, where Ned had been born. Well before the last series of her performances started, a court officially awarded her the custody of the young man whose name now would be Edwin Cushman.

In a great surge of maternal hopefulness, Charlotte wrote to Ned promising to let him make his own choice about his future education. In her mind she already envisioned him attending some outstanding school near London, coming to spend his weekends with her at the home she would make for him in one of the city's most select areas. When Ned replied gratefully, but let Auntie into his secret dream of gaining admission to the United States Naval Academy at Annapolis, Auntie suppressed her own disappointment.

During a few free days she journeyed down to Washington to make an appointment with New York's Senator William Seward, whom she had gotten to know years ago in Albany. Would the Senator do his utmost to insure her adopted son's admission to Annapolis? Miss Cushman need not worry, Senator Seward told her. Then Charlotte consoled herself about losing Ned's companionship during the four years he would spend in Maryland. Was it not fortunate, she asked herself, that she had the connections to make sure Ned achieved any goal he set for himself?

While her mind was occupied with the new possibilities life now held for her, Charlotte doggedly continued raking in dollars. But the end was in sight. If she truly intended to give up the stage forever at the conclusion of this tour, her booking agent told her, the only sensible course would be to schedule grand farewells in each of the major cities.

Did he mean going back to *Cincinnati*? Oh, not that steamy heat again! Nor would she willingly face the gales of Chicago and Buffalo even in May. In Buffalo during the preceding December she had frightened Sallie and Matilda by her intensity, on leaving the theater one icy night, as she clutched her neck. "These winds cut my throat!" she groaned.

No, she need not suffer the hardships of another westward journey, her agent assured her. But Philadelphia, New York, and Boston— each would repay her amply if it was advertised that Miss Cushman's positively final appearances in each metropolis could be witnessed during a particular few weeks.

Nerving herself for this final push, Charlotte summoned up an amazing magnetism. Her voice, her eyes, her gestures mesmerized every audience until, in New York, on the night of May 15, 1852, she bowed with a special fervor as she ended her last performance on any stage—or so she had convinced herself. In her dressing room she confessed to Matilda and Sallie, "I am weary beyond description."

One more chore—but a pleasant one—remained. On a crowded pier Charlotte easily spied Ned descending the gangway of the ship that had brought him from Liverpool, for her boy had grown tall since she had last seen him. Assuming her own new role as mother, she escorted him to Annapolis and saw him safely installed in his midshipman's quarters. She would miss him, of course, and yet the prospect of guiding him during the years to come lightened her sadness as she kissed him good-bye.

Only a series of business details detained her in America another several weeks. Throughout her career Charlotte had never lacked friends who were men of standing, capable of giving her the best financial advice. She had finished with earning money now, and she had a sizable fortune; it would enable her to live in the style she relished, if it was invested wisely. Upon the recommendation of advisers she trusted, she put most of her assets into real estate parcels bound to increase in value.

As soon as such matters were attended to, the famous Miss Cushman—on July 16, 1852, a week before her thirty-sixth birthday—embarked in New York with Matilda and Sallie on the steamship *Asia,* bound for Europe. Ahead of her was a wonderful life of leisure. And what glowing plans she had made for enjoying her retirement!

More Farewells

THOUGH Charlotte felt a strong patriotism, it had never seriously occurred to her to spend her retirement in the United States. Oh, she would surely visit her native land from time to time, but despite its increasing size—now it stretched all the way to the Pacific—and the increasing sophistication of its eastern cities, by comparison with Europe it was still raw and uncivilized, lacking the gracious standard of living she had come to appreciate. Besides, the rest of her family had irrevocably settled in England.

Thus she had chosen a ship bound for Liverpool, where she celebrated her carefree new status by staying several weeks at Rose Hill Hall. There she gave Susan a firsthand report about Ned's extraordinarily handsome appearance in his midshipman's uniform, and became better acquainted with her sister's three adorable little girls. In the process, the underlying reason for the less than perfect rapport between the Cushman sisters could not be overlooked because it was Susan's beauty that had won her such enviable domestic bliss.

Through all Charlotte's triumphs, her own longing for a pretty face had been buried only slightly below her surface assurance. Quite recently, in Cincinnati, she had astonished a young actress who playfully asked Miss Cushman to confess any unsatisfied ambition. "I would rather be a pretty woman," Charlotte had said with surprising passion, "than anything else in this wide, wide world."

If merely seeing Susan had to stir jealousy in Charlotte—for the younger sister, at the age of thirty, seemed more beautiful than ever—the duty call that Charlotte paid on her mother as soon as she reached London made her feel much worse. The neighborhood of narrow, ugly, brownish houses where Mary Eliza had chosen to settle might be respectable enough, but to Charlotte it was terribly depressing. Then her first sight of her aging mother in nearly three years tore her heart with love and sorrow.

No matter what hurts remained from the past, Charlotte forgave and forgot them because the wrinkled old lady who glumly opened the door to her deserved only pity. Though Charlotte wished she could make her mother happier, it was impossible. Any comfort that money could buy, Charlotte would gladly provide for her mother, but nothing, at this late date, could change Mary Eliza's intense disapproval of her elder daughter.

Still, Charlotte was too pleased by her own high position to remain depressed by family woes. Matilda had come directly from Liverpool to London, since she and Susan did not get on well. Rejoining loyal Matilda and taking up the social whirl that again seemed utterly delightful, Charlotte even bought herself an expensive saddle horse for spirited rides in the park every afternoon. But she hardly had time to get used to these joys of leisure before autumn signaled the real start of her retirement.

Then she and Matilda, accompanied by the faithful Sallie, who had turned into a veritable major general when it came to moving mountains of luggage, went to Paris. Charlotte plunged into sight-seeing, but she also had another objective. For the first time in her life, she bought herself a splendid personal wardrobe, including elegant hostess gowns of black velvet and lavender silk, befitting the plan that had been hatched, of all places, in Boston.

There Charlotte had learned that some of the most culturally minded of Americans had taken to spending their winters amid the glorious antiquities of Rome. Besides its wealth of historical and art treasures, this city in the heart of Italy also boasted a moderate climate allowing roses to bloom in December. Furthermore, owing to the vagaries of international monetary exchange, any citizen of the United States possessing only a middling hoard of dollars could live palatially, with servants galore, renting a large and elaborate apartment, carved out of some duke's palace, for less than the price of a two-room flat in Boston or New York.

Thus it was to Rome that Charlotte, Matilda, and Sallie were going, in the hope of setting a pattern for many happy winters. They would not be among strangers, obliged to depend on making acquaintances who spoke a foreign language. Not merely in Boston, but also in various other cities on her tour, Charlotte had attracted lively admirers who would be joining her in Rome. As the young woman who signed her newspaper articles Grace Greenwood put it, they would comprise a notable company of "jolly female bachelors." It went without saying that the fabulously successful Charlotte Cushman would be the center of their Roman holiday.

In the charming apartment that Charlotte rented, Grace and another talented young lady—vivacious Harriet Hosmer, from a Boston suburb, who aimed to be a sculptress—settled comfortably, just as they had all hoped. Charlotte held Saturday evening receptions for the American community in Rome. During the week Grace wrote, and Harriet took sculpting lessons from a master, and Matilda sulked because there was nothing she could do or say to equal the exciting activities of Charlotte's new friends.

As for Charlotte herself, she gloried in the vistas of Rome, spending her mornings sight-seeing on foot and her afternoons galloping out into the lush Italian countryside. In between, she kept up an active correspondence with dozens of friends, including her American business advisers. "You kindly offer me some silver mine shares," she wrote to one of them. "Any thing that you will let me take I shall be confident in and thankful for." Evenings, she wore her new silk and velvet gowns at gatherings of American or English acquaintances, who frequently asked her to entertain them by reciting verse; she also sang a little, enchanting almost everybody by rendering comic Irish songs in her humorous Irish brogue. But she, all too soon, was utterly bored by so much leisure, though she refused to admit it.

Back in England, after the heat of May had emptied Rome of its foreign colony, Charlotte felt reinvigorated by London's bustle. Then as she traveled about, visiting Susan and also numerous friends with lovely country homes, she found herself everywhere being quizzed with flattering questions. Why must she continue to deprive audiences of her great talent? Could she not reconsider—and return to the stage?

By autumn Charlotte needed little coaxing. Even the timid Matilda had taken courage to attempt another career of her own, editing a small magazine, and Charlotte was relieved to have her off her hands. With only herself to please, she let it be understood that an attractive offer might tempt her. After all, she had never said she would not act again in Europe; her grand farewells had been confined to America.

So in January 1854 Charlotte resumed playing Lady Macbeth and her other starring roles all over the British Isles. Though she had grown rather stout to be a convincing Romeo, she let managers persuade her that she could still draw profitable assemblages of admirers, even though her tights fit a bit snugly. The managers were not mistaken. Charlotte made more money—and she felt alive again. How could she have imagined that mere aimless pleasure-seeking could satisfy her?

With her new serenity, she smoothed over her troubles with Matilda at least temporarily. But the main reason she was glad she had given up a second Roman winter was that she found it possible to help Susan through a frightful tragedy. Charlotte spent several weeks consoling her sister in Liverpool when Susan's frail little Ida died in the spring of 1854.

For the next several years Charlotte continued acting in Britain, though she spread out her engagements so that she could visit Susan often and also spend weeks at a time resting at health resorts. When Ned sent word that on his graduation cruise from Annapolis he would have some time at a French port, Charlotte joyously arranged to meet him. Their reunion gave her immense pleasure and pride—what a fine young man Ned had become!

But seeing her son stirred a sort of worry Charlotte had thought she would never feel again. For some of her American investments were yielding less than she had hoped. To be able to help Ned, if he decided to resign from the Navy in favor of a civilian career, and also to make absolutely certain she would not have to stint on her own expenses, it struck Charlotte—in 1857—that, perhaps, she might once again shake the American money tree.

By then, Charlotte and Matilda had finally ended their long association. Charlotte's irrepressible enthusiasms for other friends, and Matilda's feeling that in some way she must win plaudits herself, had made the break inevitable. But no sooner had Matilda disappeared from Charlotte's life than another shy woman, with an unusual talent, filled the gap. Emma Stebbins from Poughkeepsie, New York, had a flair for sculpting clay, though personally she had been going through life assuming, only partly in jest, that a lion was always waiting near her path to chew her up. Charlotte's dauntless enjoyment as she kept that imaginary lion from harming Emma soon made them decide to spend their lives together.

So Emma accompanied Charlotte on what might have been a rather embarrassing tour of the United States during the late 1850s. Five years earlier, the posters outside the theaters where Miss Cushman had played her final weeks had said POSITIVELY FAREWELL APPEAR-ANCE. But managers and audiences had learned to take such proclamations by popular performers with many grains of salt. Charlotte's first series of bookings along the Atlantic coast quickly sold out, even though the people who bought the tickets behaved the way families often did. While they cheered the famous Miss Cushman with warm applause, they did some murmuring, too. "Our Charlotte has put on some weight," they said.

Still, the tour was a great success financially. Playing fourteen nights in New Orleans, Charlotte raked in more than five thousand dollars, a spectacular sum for the era. At that rate, she cannily figured, supposing that she could keep up the pace uninterruptedly over an entire year, she would be rewarded with almost twice the salary of the President of the United States.

She very nearly did keep up the pace—for two years. Yet she worked incredibly hard, despite often gruesome travel and living conditions, demonstrating once more that intensity was her main characteristic. After facing an unresponsive audience one evening, which her best efforts had failed to stir, Charlotte furiously strode offstage as the curtain descended, her deep voice throbbing as she cried out to Sallie, "Oh, I am dead and buried!" Worst of all, she was often obliged to play opposite inexperienced local actors whose blunders made her tear her hair. No wonder her throat again pained her and her limbs ached with exhaustion. Nevertheless, she carried on night after night, until the two years had accomplished their financial purpose.

Weary as she was, Charlotte made no pledges this time about retiring. By now she knew herself well enough to realize that she could not stand endless leisure and—she honestly admitted it—she needed the tonic of audience applause as a sort of medicine to keep her from turning short-tempered. But part of the reason for the extreme rigor of this American tour was that she, in fact, would soon be giving up performing—apart from an occasional short engagement in London or, perhaps, Liverpool.

She made this decision solely for the sake of Emma Stebbins. It seemed to Charlotte that Emma, as a sculptress who had already demonstrated real talent, could reach the heights of *her* career only by studying and working in the world's leading center of her art. As

Charlotte knew, Rome was that mecca for sculpture. To foster Emma's progress, Charlotte—at the age of forty-two—planned on spending every winter, thenceforth, in Rome.

She would feel amply rewarded, she assured Emma, if her own efforts provided an appropriate setting in which Emma's talent could flower. And it was not beyond the realm of possibility that Ned, too, might be encouraged to settle in Rome. With these two dear ones to look after, Charlotte felt sure the boredom that had soured her first Roman experience could easily be conquered. Knowing what to expect now, she would occupy herself most happily collecting works of art as well as visiting celebrities, Charlotte assured her friend.

Again, her return to Europe started with a relaxing stay at Rose Hill Hall. Seated in Susan's magnificent garden, talking over Ned's latest idea of leaving the Navy to join a private shipping company, Charlotte felt a new ease as she and her sister chatted companionably. Could it be that the signs of aging Susan displayed—a dimming of her lovely glow, a sort of fading, now that she was thirty-six—might at last dissipate Charlotte's envy and make them real friends?

But this fading, unfortunately, proved to be a symptom of serious illness. Later in the autumn, while Charlotte and Emma were getting settled in their elegant Roman home, Susan mysteriously grew weaker until there could be no doubting that she had some disease the medical science of the day could not even diagnose. Yet not until April did an alarming telegram reach Charlotte in Rome. It happened that Ned was visiting then, and the message was directed to him, too. COME AT ONCE, it said. For Susan's husband had concluded there was no hope.

By train and then ship, Ned and Auntie hurried to see his real mother. They were almost too late. Susan lay in a coma, broken only by occasional gasping for breath. Unable to comprehend the seriousness of the situation, Charlotte asked the doctor when he expected some improvement. "She is going very fast," the doctor replied. Charlotte waited several seconds until she could trust her voice. "You don't mean to say she is dying?" The doctor nodded.

It took several weeks, though, until, on May 12, 1859, the thirty-seven-year-old Susan died. Shocked out of rationality, Charlotte tried then to make amends for any lapses in the past by squandering a ridiculous sum of money on buying a special funeral carriage in which she and Ned and the stunned Mary Eliza followed Susan's body to the cemetery.

It may be that Charlotte's extremity of grief stemmed from her realization of a bitter truth on reading the obituary notice about Susan in the Liverpool *Daily Post*. For the paper dwelt more on Charlotte's fame than on Susan herself. Referring to Miss Charlotte Cushman, the article said, "When the gifted lady who bears that name took first rank in the first class of her profession, her sister, Miss Susan Cushman, shone like a vision on the same boards with her." Only after praising the elder sister fulsomely did the paper go on to say that, if theatergoers regretted the younger sister's departure from the stage, her "high qualities which fascinated the audience blessed a happy home."

Even in death, Charlotte had to realize, Susan received merely second billing. That the paper also called Susan "dignified" and "accomplished" meant almost nothing. Sadder and wiser, Charlotte returned to Rome—and nearly another seventeen years of an emptier life, now that she no longer had a sister to be envied by and to envy.

Yet Charlotte made a new sort of name for herself in Rome, winter after winter, helping other, younger women who were only in a broader sense her sisters. As a sort of unofficial business agent, she arranged for American tourists who craved artistic possessions to purchase works of sculpture or paintings by Emma Stebbins and other women working there. Though the idea of a "female network," functioning to give young women the moral and practical support of already successful members of their sex, would not become a popular subject for feminist discussion until another century elapsed, in effect Charlotte Cushman established just such a network.

Intermittently, she returned to acting a season or two, notably during 1863 when she went home and gave a series of performances for the benefit of Civil War wounded. Otherwise she lived mostly out of the limelight in Rome or London, amassing art treasures, spoiling her grown-up adopted son and later his children, and also making enemies among Rome's male arbiters of taste by her energetic efforts in furtherance of female careers. Then, in the spring of 1869, she made a fatal discovery.

At first, she was so terrified by the lump she found in her breast that she could not speak of it. For Charlotte had deeply dreaded cancer ever since her childhood experience of watching the suffering of her beloved grandmother. But the passage of all these years had taught Charlotte to face every sort of test without flinching, and soon her courage reasserted itself.

Then she told Emma what she had found, and her self-effacing friend proved to have absorbed more than a little of Charlotte's decisive firmness during their years together. Now it was Emma who insisted that, from now on, Charlotte must follow her advice. That led to a trip to London, where a famous physician confirmed Charlotte's own diagnosis but said a surgeon in Scotland had been achieving some cures by radical surgery, removing the affected breast.

In those early days of inadequate painkilling medication, the operation was a harrowing experience. At the age of fifty-three Charlotte survived it, but even before her months of recuperation were over, it became clear that she had not been cured. Under her arm other tiny lumps had begun growing.

Nevertheless, Charlotte conquered her fear. If Emma would not mind leaving Rome and her own career, Charlotte proposed returning home to America, not to die—but to live to the fullest whatever time remained. In fact, she wished to resume acting! Only on stage, she explained, could she possibly forget her own pain and perhaps even give some pleasure to other people.

Of course Emma agreed. With the ever-faithful Sallie, she accompanied Charlotte on what they all realized must be her last crossing of the ocean. Landing in New York in the autumn of 1870, they made their way first to Newport, Rhode Island, which Charlotte had chosen some years earlier as the place where she would make her home if she ever left Europe. Its picturesque seaside setting had pleased her even more than the congenial company the town afforded. Besides, as she wrote to a friend, Newport had "the most charming climate on our side of the water; its sea fogs soften the skin, take out all the wrinkles. . . ."

During the next few months Charlotte arranged for the construction of an elaborate villa in which she would spend her summers. Space had to be provided for her Italian art collection and also for Ned and his wife and children—her three precious grandchildren—now settled in Boston, thanks to her generosity. Though Ned was dabbling in business, surely he and his family would join her at Newport during the warm months. Only after seeing the walls of her villa begin rising did Charlotte depart to start consulting theater managers.

In the next six years the eminent Miss Cushman capped her career amazingly. Only her friends were aware, for a time, of the disease sapping her strength. Onstage Charlotte did miraculously forget her pain; the thunder of applause restored her, at least temporarily, to the glow of perfect health.

The time came, though, when acting became too strenuous, and then a round of grand farewell appearances stirred orgies of emotion in New York and Philadelphia and Boston. By then the nature of Charlotte's illness had become known, and this added an extra poignancy to her last performances. There were special ceremonies in each city after her final bows. Odes celebrating Miss Cushman were read by leading poets, and the mayors of each city presented enormous bouquets.

But nobody had counted on Charlotte's extraordinary stamina. Following another summer in Newport, surrounded by grandchildren and hordes of guests, she found it would be easier to resume traveling around the country again than to stay home and suffer. Though her performances now were "readings" rather than full-scale plays, she never stopped winning applause until, in the autumn of 1875, the course of her disease obliged her to undergo a series of treatments that doctors told her might prove helpful.

It was, fittingly, in her birthplace of Boston that she spent the ensuing winter. Occupying a suite of rooms at the Parker House— the quarters had been made especially comfortable for Charles Dickens during his recent American tour—Charlotte patiently endured her treatments every morning. Afternoons, while Emma and Sallie hovered protectively, she held court for admirers.

On the twelfth of February Charlotte felt a need for exercise and took a stroll through the corridors of the hotel. Exposed to a draft, she caught cold; pneumonia developed. Around the clock, newspaper reporters stood downstairs awaiting bulletins about the condition of the famed Miss Cushman. On February 18, 1876, the word they had been expecting was conveyed to them. At the age of fifty-nine America's most noted actress had died peacefully.

Her funeral was as dramatic as her life. A parade of students from the Boston grammar school named in her honor led a two-hour procession of mourners to the Mount Auburn Cemetery. As a leading journalist wrote, "No other woman of our day—in America at least— was as well known to so many people." The exception he surely had in mind was England's Queen Victoria.

And for several decades after Charlotte's death no other grave in the Boston area's leading cemetery attracted more visitors. Gradually, though, those who remembered her on the stage died, too, and her name was forgotten. It was part of the magic of her art, in her era, that it had to be seen firsthand—nothing like a videotape could capture it for posterity. Thus, inevitably, the fame of Charlotte Cushman faded until, a century later, she would be almost as unknown as her sister Susan.

· III ·

Emily Dickinson
and
Lavinia Dickinson

Joseph in Amherst

DOES the name Joseph Bardwell Lyman sound familiar? Most probably not, because he died more than a hundred years ago without ever having made the grand splash he had foreseen during his youth. But thanks to the saving habit of several generations of his relatives, boxes full of his old letters were preserved in a New Hampshire attic until the 1960s—when a professor read them, and marveled. As a result, we now know a little more about Emily Dickinson, whose life mystifies almost as many people as her poetry captivates. Also we know quite a lot, at last, about her sister.

Before the discovery of the Lyman letters, Lavinia Dickinson had seemed merely a typical New England spinster who happened to be in a position to protect and serve her greatly gifted elder sister. Poor Vinnie! Even her adored Emily once flippantly described her as "happy with her duties, her pussies, and her posies," and this verdict stuck. We must put it out of our minds, though, now that a fairer estimate is possible—owing to Joseph.

He was, to start with, a school friend of Emily and Vinnie's elder brother, Austin. In February 1844, from the Williston Seminary, a boarding academy for boys in western Massachusetts, Joseph wrote one of the earliest of those hoarded messages that would turn up more than a century later, informing his family of an invitation to visit Austin's home in the nearby town of Amherst. This new acquaintance, he carefully noted, was the son of the Honorable E. Dickinson, Treasurer of Amherst College.

It is easy to understand why Joseph was impressed by worldly status. The youngest of a large and fatherless family, he lived on a farm one step from actual poverty. How he managed to be sent to Williston cannot be explained, except that his every letter pulses with ambitious fervor.

Presumably, he did go home with Austin that February when he was just four months past his fourteenth birthday; the record he left sometimes only suggests what occurred, without providing any details. But at that point Vinnie—born on February 28, 1833—would have been barely eleven, and Emily—who had begun her strange and wonderful existence on December 10, 1830—had just recently turned thirteen. Thus it might be safe to assume that Austin's friend hardly noticed "the Dickinson girls," as he would soon be referring to them.

Still, they undoubtedly noticed him, for Joseph, as others besides himself could not fail to see, was a very good-looking young man. He had curly dark hair that refused to stay tamed by a comb and, despite the shyness he constantly bewailed, his manners were extremely appealing. Resembling a young Greek god, he always seemed to need reassurance, which females of every age were glad to provide. Yet he got along well with males, too, so Joseph became a frequent guest at the large, white-shingled Dickinson establishment behind its trim picket fence on Pleasant Street in Amherst.

If Joseph was awed by the Dickinsons' home, that was exactly what the Honorable Edward Dickinson intended. He owed the title, it must be explained, to having been elected to a few terms in the Massachusetts legislature. But though there had been respected bearers of this name in the Amherst area since the late 1600s, only Edward's father—the grandfather of Emily and Lavinia—had distinguished himself beyond the immediate vicinity. Samuel Fowler Dickinson had gained statewide renown by taking the lead in founding Amherst College, and, as a prosperous lawyer, he almost single-handedly supported this local competitor to Harvard and Yale through its initial growing pains. Still, old Samuel had learned the meaning of failure.

After he had every right to expect that his pet project had been well launched, business conditions throughout the country took a sudden slide. Mortgaging the homestead he had built for his own family—reputedly, Amherst's first house of solid brick—Samuel had used the money to carry the college through the hard times, but in the process he lost his own elegant house. Almost penniless, he moved out to Ohio for a fresh start just about when his granddaughter Lavinia was born. It was too late, though; he died within a few years.

However, his eldest son—Emily and Lavinia's father—doggedly set himself the task of repairing the damage to his family's good name. He, too, was a lawyer, tall, imposing, and austere. Indeed, Edward Dickinson's whole outlook on life, no less than his appearance, made him a remarkable throwback to New England's original Puritans. Whether he actually did behave with such severity that he deserves the reputation he has acquired in most of the legends about his famous daughter—whether he really was a terrible domestic tyrant—is a question we shall be considering shortly. Now we need to note only that, well before young Joseph Lyman's first visit to Amherst, Edward Dickinson had already become the community's leading citizen. "Squire" Dickinson, he was called, in the style of old England's deference to its rural gentry.

As the college's treasurer, the Squire had revived its prosperity, while also restoring his own family's prestige. Though it would be another decade before the opportunity arose for him to buy back the solid brick homestead his father had constructed, in the interim he had settled his wife and three children almost as impressively on Pleasant Street. Even if their house was made of wood and lacked the extensive acreage surrounding the brick dwelling on the outskirts of the village, its rooms were spacious; its rear garden provided ample privacy.

So the Squire's son—Austin, born on April 16, 1829, was six months older than Joseph—fliply referred to his home as "the mansion." And Joseph, comparing it with his own family's rude farmhouse, could only agree. Yet the superior atmosphere of the Dickinsons' daily existence, the lively talk at their dinner table about books and local happenings, stirred Joseph emotionally more than the mere trappings of affluence did. He would always feel a glow of warmth, remembering how he had been included in what seemed to him a sort of magic circle. Even allowing for his lifelong tendency to dramatize his every experience, it is still hard to read his boyish memories of his early welcome in Amherst without beginning to doubt those stories that spread after Emily Dickinson's death, concerning the fierce tyranny of her father.

For Joseph would turn into a journalist of some success, employed by several of New York City's leading newspapers; he would prove himself quite an acute observer. Thus his firsthand testimony merits attention, especially because he continued his visits until he did notice the Dickinson girls. Although his disclosures regarding some of Emily's comments to him, as well as his general impressions of her home life during this period, have been of most interest to scholars, we are going to concentrate on his relationship with Vinnie—a story bound to change many opinions about proper young ladies in staid New England around the middle of the 1800s.

It started when Joseph, at sixteen, spent an entire term as a member of the Dickinson household. The Squire, for some unknown reason, required his son's presence in Amherst, and asked his son's friend to keep him company, the theory being that they would study together, covering the work they were missing at Williston. No doubt they did pore over books diligently. Austin, despite a streak of singularity symbolized by his copper-red head, displayed sufficient seriousness to please his father. But it was spring, and Joseph's daydreams inevitably drifted toward Austin's pretty sister.

Not Emily. That April of 1846 Emily was fifteen and, clearly, no beauty. Wispy thin, with a face of the extreme pallor that often accompanies reddish chestnut hair—its glossy color was lovely, but she brushed every strand into a tight knot at the back of her neck—she could give nobody the notion of calling her pretty, though the oddest, shrewdest, funniest ideas kept emerging in a breathless rush from her prodigiously busy brain. With her, Joseph pored over the German dictionary her father had provided to help her learn the language. Also, Joseph and Emily occasionally sat up late, philosophizing after all the others had taken their candles and gone to bed.

It was Vinnie, very pretty at thirteen, and pert, too, who flirtily enchanted Joseph. Small and slightly plump, she had dark eyes that sparkled as she smiled at him. Soon he found himself walking to school with her every morning, then awaiting her on the gravel path outside the building every afternoon. He always carried her books while they ambled back and forth along Pleasant Street.

The feelings that began agitating Joseph and Vinnie during this spring of 1846 did not fade when he left Amherst, in spite of the ending of one stage of his life a few months later, and the opening of an enormous new challenge. That autumn, while Austin remained at home to start attending Amherst College, Joseph entered Yale, where he somehow paid his fees and earned a diploma, though it would take him nearly five years. Throughout these years he remained in touch with the Dickinsons.

Thus he knew that Emily, for all her peculiar spurts of fear at the approach of strangers, also went away to school. Among her friends— and she made the warmest of friendships with those she trusted—she could joke even about her plain appearance. "I am growing handsome very fast indeed!" she had exuberantly written to a girl she liked immensely. "I expect I shall be the belle of Amherst when I reach my

17th year." Having reached it, though, she accepted her father's decision in favor of sending her to the Mount Holyoke Female Seminary, but not very happily. To say that her concern over her lack of beauty lay behind Emily's discomfort is much too simple in the case of someone of her complexity. Still there is no escaping the fact that, on her home grounds where she had demonstrated how exceptionally clever she really was, regardless of her unprepossessing exterior, the young Emily thoroughly relished companionship.

She did not, however, thrive at Mount Holyoke. Intellectually, she probably gained from her exposure to the most rigorous higher education then available to women, even if her own reading at home might have taught her all she needed. But, socially, she felt lost. When flurries of valentines descended on the other girls, she only slightly disguised her sense of apartness, ruefully writing to Austin, who was then her closest confidant, "your *highly accomplished & gifted elder sister* is entirely overlooked." On another occasion, on which some entertainment had been made available: "Almost all of the girls went & I enjoyed the solitude finely."

But Mount Holyoke's location, just ten miles from Amherst, offered some consolation. Although strict rules forbade weekend absences by any student, family visits to the seminary were allowed, and Emily lived for the sight of her relatives. So she was not sorry to develop a bad cough in her second semester, causing her father to send Austin to escort her home. On her return a month later, she knew the worst was over—her father had promised that she need not endure a second year where conformity was expected of her. For Miss Mary Lyon, the school's founder, had very definite ideas about religion and other subjects that Emily could not accept; she had to think for herself.

Back in Amherst, her daily life was certainly restricted in many ways that would seem oppressive a century later to any young woman with even a much less intensely independent mind. Emily wore cumbersome long skirts as a matter of course, and she did her share of household chores, mainly baking bread. Yet she felt safe on Pleasant Street, safe and free to think her own thoughts.

A daguerrotype of Emily Dickinson made while she was a student at Mount Holyoke. This is the only portrait that has been found.

Lavinia Dickinson about the age of twenty.

Though she and Vinnie shared the same bedroom, Vinnie's kind heart infallibly told her when Emily needed solitude. For Emily had already perceived a need to put down some of her thoughts on paper, mostly in letters to cousins or close friends. Often Vinnie shut her eyes and went to sleep while Emily sat up by candlelight, writing on and on in her tiny script.

But after the Squire's younger daughter turned sixteen, he decided that she, too, should have a year away at school. As Joseph surely was informed, Vinnie went farther than Emily had, beyond Boston to an academy in the town of Ipswich that was almost as highly regarded as Mount Holyoke. Possibly, Emily's experience had made Miss Lyon seem too much an ogre for the less studious of the Dickinson girls to contend with. Also, the fact that Vinnie's best friend— Jennie Hitchcock, daughter of the president of Amherst College— would be going with her undoubtedly made the greater distance no deterrent. Still, it is easy to conclude that Vinnie's own spirit of adventure was the main factor determining the choice of Ipswich, fully a hundred and twenty-five miles from Amherst.

Unlike Emily, she loved to travel. Twice before, she had paid extended visits in Boston, which she had vastly enjoyed. While there, she had stayed with the Aunt Lavinia after whom she had been named, and, to Vinnie, this aunt was the warmest, liveliest, most affectionate woman in the world. Aunt Lavinia was the younger sister of Emily and Vinnie's mother. So, at last, we must confront the enigma of Squire Dickinson's insignificant wife.

Born Emily Norcross, the daughter of a well-off farmer in a village near Amherst, she had been "amiable," possessed of "good taste" and a "thorough knowledge of every aspect of domestic economy." Thus Edward Dickinson had described her when he was courting her. At that period, other surviving evidence shows, she had an active, busy life, by no means confined to household duties, for she attended singing school, went to lectures on chemistry or history, and took part in many church-related projects.

After her marriage something happened. Perhaps voluntarily, finding herself the wife of a man with extremely definite convictions on every topic, she effaced herself until she became hardly more than a mere domestic presence, flailing at carpets during spring cleaning and fretfully urging guests to try the rocking chair, though the armchair might be more comfortable, or would a seat farther from the fire be better? She also produced excellent crullers and custards, Joseph testified. Until a later period, however, she appears to have had little rapport with either of her daughters, not even writing to them while they were away at school, instead just relaying her love via her son or her husband.

Again unlike Emily, Vinnie had great fun at her school. Because she shared a room with Jennie Hitchcock, who kept up a correspondence with Austin then, we have a cheerful picture of Vinnie rising above the dour lectures of some of their teachers. After morning prayers, Jennie related, a teacher she identified as Mr. C. regularly reminded the girls that they were not placed in this world to *have a good time*. Others spoke about *restraining* their *feelings*. "Now such things would crush me," Jennie told Austin, "were it not for your dear sister Vinnie. Fortunately," Jennie explained, "she still retains her ability to 'take off' people. You have seen her enough to know how well she does it. I assure you it is a real comfort."

Vinnie had a real gift as a mimic, a forthright way of expressing herself. Yet the warm and lively young Vinnie has often been overlooked in biographies of her sister. Instead she is portrayed as rather forbidding, because family letters from this period emphasize the brisk, practical side of her nature.

That is not surprising. Upon returning home from Ipswich, Vinnie naturally assumed increasing responsibility for making the household run smoothly because her mother's health had begun failing. And Emily kept so busy with her thinking and her baking that ordinary errands were a trouble Vinnie gladly spared her. Even so, in 1851, when Vinnie was eighteen, she saw her own future as rosy indeed, and she showed no signs of turning into a sharp-voiced old maid.

We can be positive of this, for in March of that year Joseph Lyman, at twenty-one, finished his Yale studies and, before venturing to seek his fortune, he paid an extended visit to "that charming second home of mine in Amherst." In bundles of his letters that would be discovered more than a hundred years afterward—letters to his mother, to his brothers and sisters, and to another friend—Joseph set down incontrovertible proof of Vinnie's softer, warmer side. Beyond question, she not only fell deeply in love with him when she was eighteen; she also let him know her feelings. And he did not rebuff her.

In Amherst then, as in New England to this day, spring comes not by the calendar but, most preciously, it arrives unannounced. A sudden warm spell melts the snow, revealing tiny green spears of crocus leaves, and if the weather remains mild, bright little yellow and light purple and white flowers may open, while taller golden daffodils push upward toward the sun, even though everybody knows April may still bring a blizzard. The March of 1851, during which Joseph stayed on Pleasant Street, was exceptionally favorable.

Out in the garden, one balmy evening, Joseph exultantly was moved to spout from Shakespeare's *Romeo and Juliet*. "Lady," Joseph proclaimed to Vinnie, "by yonder blessed moon I vow . . ." And very soon they were kissing as they stood among the crocus flowers. "*They* and the daffodils and the little arbutus had left their sweetness upon her lips!" Joseph would tell his friend.

It happened repeatedly, outdoors and also in the family sitting room after everyone else had gone upstairs. ". . . I remember," Joseph would write, "how she used to take her little red ottoman and with almost childish grace come and set it close by my chair on the left side of me and lay her arm across my lap and put the book she was reading up against me and look from its pages into my face & read to me . . ." Also:

> I was very happy in Vinnie's arms—very happy. She sat
> in my lap and pulled the pins from her long soft chestnut
> hair and tied the long silken mass around my neck and kissed

me again & again. She was always at my side clinging to my
arm. . . . Her skin was very soft . . . I was very, very happy
with her.

Through it all, Vinnie trusted Joseph not to forget that she was a
respectable young lady, and he did not forget it. Yet they both understood that playing "spoony" so often and with such heat meant that,
at least unofficially, they were engaged to be married. Vinnie guile-
lessly assumed Joseph was just as overjoyed by the prospect of having
her as his wife as she was in picturing him as her husband.

His words and his actions gave her not the slightest reason to doubt
his love. Then, on the next to the last day before his departure, a
lively party of young people drove out into the countryside for a
traditional excursion to taste freshly boiled maple syrup. Seated beside
Vinnie in one of the carriages on their way out to the woods, Joseph
felt her affection enveloping him with an aura even softer than the
balmy air. Suddenly he turned thoughtful.

After the carriages halted near a clearing where a great kettle bubbled
over a blazing fire, the Amherst group spent all afternoon rambling
about the woods, laughing and talking. Joseph found himself making
a point of accompanying Emily a good deal, then Jennie Hitchcock,
until toward dusk he strolled off by himself and sat down alone on a
rock beside a spring.

Unbidden memories of his own youth on his family's farm, when
he had been just a poor boy with no prospects, who was obliged to
do such heavy work as lugging buckets of maple sap, crowded his
mind as he sat there. How much had changed since then! Through
his own efforts, he had already raised himself amazingly. Who could
have expected that poor, friendless youth to graduate from Yale?

Then his thoughts turned toward his favorite subject of his future.
Carrying a generous letter of recommendation from the president of
Yale, he was planning to seek a teaching post in the South because,
according to all he had heard, a young man with his education and

ability, not least his ability to win friends wherever he went, should have no difficulty finding a suitable position there. Of course, teaching would be just a means toward some higher end. By living spartanly, saving most of what he earned, he calculated that within two years he would be in a position to come North again and study law. Which might lead . . . who could tell to what heights?

Just as Joseph was beginning to reflect on where the frivolous-minded Vinnie might fit into his ambitious schemes, she herself appeared through a gap in the trees. Coming up to him, she took his hand and said, "Oh, Joseph, I haven't seen much of you today." In her disappointment she almost wailed that a homely fellow named Howland had been with her most of the afternoon. "But I would so much rather have been with you," she added in a tone that sounded plaintive to Joseph.

"My dear Vinnie," he said, "I thought it best under the circumstances not to pay you very marked attention before all these people. I would avoid everything like gossip."

"I know, Joseph," Vinnie said earnestly, "but I love you, and I am proud of you and of your love—I want people to know that you love me. Come, Joseph, they are all going to the carriages. Let me take your arm and we will sit together in the carriage. Oh, Joseph, *must* you go tomorrow?"

Joseph assured her that he positively must leave, but he did nothing during the brief period before his departure to change Vinnie's belief in her own glowing future. She had no doubt that in two years, when Joseph came back from the South, they would no longer make any secret of their commitment to each other. The world would know then that they were engaged to be married.

Meanwhile, on March 26, 1851, the eighteen-year-old Vinnie wrote in the little black leather "Pocket Remembrancer" that her friend Jennie had given her for a New Year's present: "Walked with Joseph. Now he is gone! Two years is a long time!"

Leave Emily Alone?

A FTER Joseph went to Natchez, where a brother of his had settled along the lower Mississippi River, life in Amherst continued its usual course. With a population of only a few hundred families, who mostly kept to the ways of the past, the town retained an almost colonial flavor. Certainly it lacked the excitement and the diversity of cities like Boston or New York.

More than a century later we might expect that Amherst College would have enlivened the community, and, to the extent of providing some public lectures as well as a staid round of receptions, it did. But the college had been founded by conservative men like Emily and Vinnie's grandfather mainly because they feared the increasing liberalism of Harvard, which they wished to counteract. So they and their successors, as late as the 1850s, concentrated on training young males of strict morality to uphold the sober old New England standards.

No wonder, then, that Vinnie found her local suitors not nearly as appealing as Joseph. Most particularly, the same boring Howland who had followed her all afternoon during the expedition out to the maple-sugaring kept calling on her, solemnly urging her to come walking or driving with him. At last, he stammered an outright proposal. Would she marry him? Vinnie did not hurt his feelings by ridiculing the idea, but her compassion stopped short of giving him—or any of the other more or less attractive swains always hanging around her— the slightest encouragement. Compared with Joseph, how dull they all seemed!

That is not to say Vinnie suffered discontent or, indeed, suffered anything else of much importance during the next several months. As her "Pocket Remembrancer" shows, she went out walking or entertained visitors continually, she sewed or ironed, she read *Harper's Magazine* and *David Copperfield*. Several times a month, at least at the beginning, she noted, "Wrote to Joseph." Presumably, she also received letters from him, but very little of their correspondence has survived.

Within the Dickinsons' home all seemed serene. By chance, in July 1851 an event occurred that gave Emily a fine opportunity to divert Austin, who was away then, trying his hand at teaching schoolboys in Boston. Describing her father's reaction on a notable occasion, she also tells us a great deal about the relationships between the members of this family.

The event was a Jenny Lind concert. The fabulous "Swedish Song-bird," since landing in New York the preceding year, had been touring the country, arousing wild enthusiasm wherever she went. When she was booked to appear in Northampton, a short carriage ride from Amherst, the Honorable Edward Dickinson found it fitting to dignify the entertainment by his presence, a conclusion his wife and two daughters had clearly helped him reach. Left to consider only his own comfort, he would have preferred remaining sensibly on Pleasant

Street during a humid evening that threatened and produced a violent thunderstorm. Still, the four of them arrived at the hall safely—Emily's witty account of their trials, and then of the actual performance, fills several pages of her tiny script. Here is just one of her inimitable sentences:

> Father sat all the evening looking *mad,* and *silly,* and yet so much amused you would have *died* a laughing—when the performers bowed, he said "Good evening Sir"—and when they retired, "very well—that will do," it was'nt *sarcasm* exactly, nor it was'nt *disdain,* it was infinitely funnier than either of those virtues, as if old Abraham had come to see the show, and thought it was all very well, but a little excess of *Monkey!*

First of all, just on the surface, we see Emily's own disdain for many rules of proper English composition, particularly her fondness for dashes. We must also notice her habit of stressing certain words, besides her use of comparison—metaphor—to etch a deeper impression than any simple description could possibly accomplish. Because Austin enjoyed her unexpected quirks, and because she delighted in making up teasing riddles, she blithely chose words or phrases with nuances that could elude anybody else.

Possibly her early confidence in her brother's admiration helps to explain why she would always write somewhat cryptically, so that ever since Emily Dickinson's poetry began being published, professors have felt impelled to offer their own interpretations of her every line. Sometimes their efforts do clear away mysteries. Frequently, though, she seems confusing merely because she crams so much meaning into such limited space. Even the above passage from a spontaneous letter, written when she was only twenty, tells us far more than might be readily apparent.

Mainly, it tells us that Emily and Austin are in the habit of laughing together over their father's gruff spoutings. This laughter does not seem to include any element of fear, let alone terror. Taken with the rest of her letter, the passage even suggests that the Squire might be just as anxious to please the females in his family, when he could do so in good conscience, as less austere husbands and fathers often are.

Not that he never lost his temper. "A storm blew up" is a phrase repeatedly, and not a bit cryptically, sprinkling the letters the Dickinson children wrote to each other in this period, so we do have grounds for believing their father's rigid notions of propriety strongly influenced all of them. No doubt his insistence on female modesty caused Emily, and Vinnie, too, to forgo curling their hair as other girls of their day did, and he objected strenuously to low-cut dresses. Yet there seems ample evidence that Squire Dickinson nevertheless allowed far greater leeway for both Emily and Vinnie than the legends indicate.

He constantly provided Emily with stimulating reading material, though he grumbled about her fondness for some literature he considered worthless. He trusted the openly flirtatious Vinnie by leaving her alone with Joseph or other obviously smitten young men, even if he raised the roof when she failed to return home at the promised hour. In short, the total record denies Edward Dickinson the label of a fierce tyrant, though he must have been a very difficult father for his son as well as his daughters.

At least a partial explanation of the difficulties emerges between the lines in another part of Emily's letter about the Jenny Lind concert, which shows that there was no easy communication among most members of this family. They might sit side by side, yet they were separated from each other's inner thoughts or feelings. Only Emily and Austin, at this period, seem to have achieved any sort of rapport.

Probably their special closeness owed much to the special circumstance of their being just eighteen months apart in age. By the time Vinnie—nearly four years younger than her brother, and a little more than two years younger than her sister—was old enough to envy their private laughter, they had become accustomed to excluding her from their joking. Thus Vinnie grew up feeling left out, but she made her own jokes.

"I think Emilie is very much improved," she wrote to Austin in the autumn of 1851. "She has really grown *fat,* if youll believe it. I am very strict with her & I shouldnt wonder if she should come out bright some time after all." Indeed, Vinnie made the best of her own bent for taking charge. If mending shirts for her brother and mailing letters for her sister earned her their gratitude, she accepted this without worrying too much about what she was missing.

Still, it is doubtful that Vinnie really deserved the inferior status that her brother and sister assigned her. Compared with Emily, it was certainly justified; not one in many million has a mind like Emily Dickinson's. And yet Austin was hardly any better equipped than Vinnie to comprehend Emily's genius. If he started out by seeming more sensitive to her meanings than Vinnie, that was mainly a matter of being the recipient of her confidences, which made him appear more perceptive than he actually was. Never, years afterward, would he appreciate the value of Emily's poetry, and, by the time her work reached public attention, Vinnie had infinitely more faith in it than Austin did.

In fact, the process whereby Vinnie gradually superseded Austin as the most important person supporting Emily's fragile tie with the world beyond Pleasant Street had already begun while Vinnie was waiting until her adored Joseph returned to claim her as his bride. Emily herself did not realize this. For those boxes of Lyman letters contain a remarkable passage in which she gave her own assessment of her father and sister. Emily wrote:

> My father seems to me often the oldest and oddest sort of a foreigner. Sometimes I say something and he stares in a curious sort of bewilderment. . . . And Vinnie, Joseph, it is so weird and so vastly mysterious, she sleeps by my side, her care is in some sort motherly, for you may remember that our amiable mother never taught us tayloring . . . so Vinnie is in the matter of raiment greatly necessary to me; and the tie is quite vital; yet if we had come up for the first

time from two wells where we had hitherto been bred her astonishment would not be greater at some things I say.

Father says in fugitive moments when he forgets the barrister & lapses into the man, says that his life has been passed in a wilderness or on an island—of late he says on an island. And so it is, for in the morning I hear his voice and methinks it comes from afar & has a sea tone & there is a hum of hoarseness about [it] & a suggestion of remoteness as far as the isle of Juan Fernandez.

So I conclude that space & time are things of the body & have little or nothing to do with our selves. My Country is Truth. Vinnie lives much of the time in the State of Regret. I like Truth—it is a free Democracy.

We must note, though, that Emily was hardly being fair to Vinnie. As to her sister's astonishment "at some things I say," in another decade Emily would ruefully admit that "All men say 'What' to me." So Vinnie's inability to understand some of Emily's remarks was scarcely surprising; it would have been truly extraordinary if she did comprehend Emily's every subtlety. More sadly, Emily's offhand comment about Vinnie and her "State of Regret" came close to cruelty.

As Emily could not help being aware, Vinnie had ample cause for regret as one year passed, and then another, without her receiving any sign that Joseph was on his way back to Massachusetts. Did he still intend to marry her? We do not know what Joseph told Vinnie herself because she destroyed all his letters to her. Still it seems likely that, for several years, he alternately raised and then dashed her hopes. It is possible to guess that he treated her with such callousness, on the basis of dozens of other letters he wrote during the 1850s.

Moving from Natchez to Nashville to New Orleans, always seeking a more promising opportunity, until he finally settled on studying law in New Orleans, Joseph vacillated even more variably about his commitment to Vinnie. Away from her enchanting presence, he quickly rediscovered how easy it was for him to draw female attention, and he kept being tempted by new flirtations. In November 1852, a year and a half after his departure from Amherst, he vowed an end to all such diversion so that he could concentrate on his career. "The Ladies I am altogather weaned from them," he assured his sister, then he added: "Poor little soft-lipped Vinnie Dickinson. She thinks I am *so* far off and Life is *so* long! So we have concluded that it was *not* one of the matches made in heaven and not to be made on Earth."

Eighteen months later, however, Joseph blandly discussed the same subject in a letter to his mother during May 1854. "You ask about my Amherst attachment," he wrote. "It is all right. Vinnie loves me and I love Vinnie and mean to marry her God willing—God and her old folks—and I have reason to think they do not object very much."

By then it was more than three years since Vinnie had seen Joseph, and, month after month, she briskly kept finding new distractions. "I feel unusually hurried just now, so many plans suggest themselves to my mind for improving the house & grounds," she wrote to Austin at Harvard Law School. Furthermore, a major change in their father's career had opened a fascinating prospect for her. Late in 1852 Edward Dickinson was elected to the national Congress, meaning that he would spend a good part of the next several years in Washington— and he wanted his wife and daughters to consider visiting him there.

While the idea of making the trip thrilled Vinnie, another emotion that had been gradually growing within her caused a conflict. For Emily in these years had increasingly preferred staying at home, even finding a reason many Sundays to avoid venturing forth to church. Their father would not insist on having her go out, whether near or far, so an arrangement of some sort would be required if she wished to remain in Amherst. And she did. What, then, should Vinnie do? In a letter to Austin she expressed her perplexity with six short words of enormous weight: "I hate to leave Emily alone."

On this occasion, however, Vinnie was prevented from sacrificing her own enjoyment by a happy combination of volunteers. Emily's dearest friend during these years of her early twenties was Susan Gilbert, a clever and ambitious young woman. Sue proved able to keep Emily company at the house on Pleasant Street, while suitable male protection was provided by a Dickinson cousin attending the college.

Thus Vinnie was free to accompany her mother all the way to Washington for a wonderfully diverting April. At the Willard Hotel, where the family boarded, the pert Miss Dickinson sometimes entertained a parlor full of visitors with her imitations of Amherst characters, such as poor old Mrs. James whose lungs were all tied up in a knot so she "haint got nothin to hitch her breath on to."

The following February, for reasons unknown, both Emily and Vinnie traveled with their mother, not only staying nearly a month in Washington but also stopping several weeks at the home of relatives in Philadelphia on their way back to Amherst. Almost nothing factual survives about this most extensive journey Emily Dickinson ever took, except one letter in which she told a friend how she and Vinnie "on one soft spring day glided down the Potomac in a painted boat," then jumped ashore, hand in hand, to explore General George Washington's "sweet Mount Vernon."

Yet the trip plays a crucial part in the legend about Emily that very soon would begin being whispered in Amherst and, after her death, would spread around the world. According to this myth, Emily met a man while she was away, with whom she instantly and irrevocably fell in love and, though he, too, lost his heart, they forever renounced each other because he already had a wife.

In Philadelphia Emily did meet a married clergyman named the Reverend Charles Wadsworth, noted for his thoughtful as well as inspiring preaching. While it is possible that she developed a passionate interest in him—her intensity led to a number of highly charged emotional involvements—there is absolutely no way of knowing the truth about her relationship with the Reverend Wadsworth. Yet every scrap of reliable evidence available suggests merely a sort of student-teacher connection carried on in letters in which Emily sought spiritual guidance and was, perhaps, helped by what amounted to private sermons.

142

Yet Vinnie's real love affair seems to have been really affected by her sojourns in the nation's capital. Her exposure to a wider society and its preoccupation with the major issue of the day eventually gave Joseph an excuse for which he had, at least unconsciously, been searching. In February 1855, almost four years after his departure from Amherst, he had not yet found the pretext he was seeking, and he wrote to his mother:

> Vinnie Dickinson continues to love me very truly and writes me beautiful letters from Washington where she is now staying with her Father. She is a Christian girl and begs me to be very good. I think her parents object to her coming South but Vinnie declares that she can never love anybody else and I think I shall go on and marry her some of these summers if we live.

Slavery, of course, was the issue most agitating Washington then, and Vinnie's father, as a Congressman from Massachusetts with its spreading abolitionism, no doubt took a dim view of having his daughter settle among slave owners. Indeed, the idea of her marrying Joseph and living in New Orleans was quite different from her original idea of marrying Joseph and living, if not in Amherst, not very far away. But it seems very likely that Joseph used slavery as a convenient escape route.

He himself had changed his mind extraordinarily about this issue. Three years earlier, he had expressed his sentiments with great force. "I do not like the South at all—and I especially hate the peculiar Institution of the Country," he told one of his brothers. "I would much prefer to live in a free or still better a Yankee State but for the present I think I could do better here." To his mother, he was even more vigorous after having managed to obtain a copy of *Uncle Tom's Cabin:*

> It is not much exaggerated . . . it is a picture of Southern Life. Mother you need not be afraid that I shall take any 30

pieces of silver for hush-money and come back to stand up for the South and Slavery. . . . Before God I declare it to be the damnedest handicraft of Satan that he ever sent out of the place of torment.

But here is the same Joseph three years later, writing to another of his relatives:

I have told Vinnie again & again that she had better forget me and let me go my way. I never asked for her love or her hand—She gave them to me and I could not but be grateful & proud of so rich a gift. *She* would go with me to New Orleans or anyplace else but I know her parents have the same invincible prejudices to the *South* that Yankees and Abolitionists generally have. For myself I am getting attached to the South. I like it & can succeed here & with the favor of God *will* succeed, if I live.

Joseph, however, failed to mention a very relevant fact in most of these letters. During his stay in Nashville he had become acquainted with an unusually strong-minded schoolteacher named Laura Baker. By no means beautiful, or even nearly as pretty as Vinnie, Laura, he soon became convinced, had a noble character. And that was what he most needed in a wife, it struck him. With a woman like her constantly guarding him against his tendency just to enjoy life, Joseph thought, his success would be far more likely to meet his own high expectations.

And this theory seemed to be proving itself. In New Orleans, spurred by Laura's long and solemn letters from Nashville, he achieved first place among his fellow law students at the University of Louisiana. By March 1856 Joseph—at last—made up his mind. Almost precisely five years to the date after he had left Vinnie in Amherst, promising to return and marry her, he wrote a long and solemn letter himself, asking Laura to become his wife.

She accepted him. Still, Joseph did not inform Vinnie of his new situation for several months and, finally, he did so only indirectly. Meanwhile, he wrote copiously and revealingly about Vinnie—he wrote and told Laura all about her. Laura was the previously mentioned "friend" to whom he confided every detail of his Amherst courtship, supposedly to show her how much his judgment had improved, besides letting her realize what a good catch he was.

It is only because Joseph told Laura about his own playing Romeo among the crocus flowers, and about the sweetness of Vinnie's kisses, that we know the sad story of Vinnie's romance, which very probably changed the whole course of her life. Between the ages of sixteen and twenty-four, she could not love any other man because Joseph was her beloved ideal. With her warm nature, it seems more than likely that another suitor might have met her favor if she had not been blinded by Joseph's curly locks and charming manners. Yet he certainly lacked courage.

When he could no longer delay making her aware of his impending marriage, he took the most cowardly way imaginable. Instead of writing to her, he wrote to Emily and, just incidentally, inquired about Vinnie, then mentioned what he intended.

Vinnie, informed thus of the end of her hopes, sent a brave letter to New Orleans that did get saved. She wrote:

> My Dear Joseph—I'm glad you are happy—Im glad you are successful there where you most desire success—I'm glad you have found a life-companion who pleases you. I wish I could see you *once more* before you are married. Our Early Love seems to me a sweet dream, I have forgotten all the bitter . . . You asked who I will marry, Joseph. I wish I knew. I have some dear friends. I have promised to decide *the* question before winter is all gone. Perhaps I may give them all up. I shall always love to hear from you, Joseph & trust you will be *good* & prosperous. God bless you! Joseph.
>
> Good bye
> Vinnie

Laura, we must add, would be left a widow with five children to finish raising by herself when Joseph died of smallpox at the age of forty-two in New York City, where he was then agricultural editor of the *Tribune*. As far as we know, he never went back to Amherst after his marriage but, even so, his effect on "the Dickinson girls" was lasting. It is not too much to say that his fickleness, over five crucial years, produced the frame of mind within which Vinnie became accustomed to making her own plans based on those few but weighty words: *I hate to leave Emily alone.*

At the Homestead

SHORTLY before Vinnie's romance collapsed, there had occurred an event of great significance to the entire Dickinson family. Following the death of an elderly Amherst gentleman, who had been occupying the brick mansion built by Edward Dickinson's father, the house went on sale. Unhesitatingly the Squire purchased it.

Then, during the autumn of 1855, he and his wife and their two daughters took up residence in the imposing structure that would always, thereafter, be referred to as the Homestead. With its brick painted a pale yellow, its front entry marked by a pillared portico, it looked down on the far end of the village's Main Street behind not just a fence of metal railing but also a tall hedge of hemlock. Its privacy was further insured by towering trees along the gravel sidewalk.

Even the meadows across the road belonged to the property, although their open expanse made them seem almost common ground. But the spacious hidden areas on both sides of the Homestead, and to its rear, provided something like a universe in miniature, invisible to any passerby. Protected as it was, it soon nurtured an enemy.

For a second house was constructed, during the ensuing year, behind the same tall hedge as the Homestead. It, too, faced Main Street, from which it could be approached through its own separate gateway. It had been built to accommodate Austin—and his bride. Since the lives of both Emily and Vinnie would be so closely interwoven with their brother's personal complications, it is necessary to backtrack to see how he happened to bring a potential source of misery into their midst.

After completing his studies at Amherst College, Austin's most practical course would have been to study law with his father. In those days entering the profession via such informal tutoring was still quite usual. Unquestionably, the Squire desired his son to join him; it was

The Dickinson Homestead in Amherst.

his deepest aim. And for a few months the son did try to learn legal practice under his father's direction.

What happened to end this association is another of those mysteries that defy the most energetic of Dickinson investigators. Presumably, it was not too serious an episode of youthful revolt, because Austin remained in friendly communication with his family after he went off to teach school for a few years. But his pay and his status were too lowly to satisfy him long, and he was not allowed to forget that local eminence as well as affluence would reward his return to work with his father in Amherst.

It must have been a sort of compromise that impelled Austin, after all, to prepare himself for a legal career but to do it at Harvard instead of resuming his apprenticeship in his father's office. During his years in Boston, though, he mulled over a further declaration of independence, such as picking up and starting out on his own in some Western state. While he was thinking along these lines, he also became involved romantically—which sealed his fate.

The young woman he almost accidentally began courting was the same Sue Gilbert who had stayed with Emily on Pleasant Street during Vinnie's first trip to Washington. It is impossible to fathom Sue's character because throughout her life she would display a bewildering variability. So it appears that she had natural gifts as an actress, besides being unusually intelligent, self-seeking, and malicious.

To be fair to her, we should note that she had had a far less secure childhood than most of her future associates. The daughter of a tavern keeper, who reputedly drank up his own profits, Sue and her sister Martha were orphaned in their early teens. Then they were shifted around to be cared for by various aunts and a married sister, scattered from Amherst to upstate New York. Yet it is hard to blame Sue's unlikable qualities on her early trauma. Martha—always called Mattie— was a year her senior and would always be as warm and gentle as Sue was cool and decisive.

Still, Sue, early and late, possessed some strange magnetism whereby she made other people feel honored by her notice. At school in Amherst with Emily, she had exerted her power to the extent that Emily, for a few years, adored her. To Sue's credit, it must be admitted that she was one of the few who understood most of Emily's riddles, and yet we must wonder whether, right from the beginning, Sue used Emily as a sort of steppingstone. After all, Emily had a brother bound to become the leading citizen of a town Sue aimed to rule, at least socially.

Though Austin himself had developed a brotherly fondness for the gentle Mattie, it was Mattie's clever sister with whom local gossip began linking him after his father was elected to Congress. How that gossip started can only be guessed. But when Austin gathered what was expected of him, flattered as well as amused, he turned his attention to Sue, who fed some buried flame of poetic feeling in him. Also, years later, he would offer the peculiarly snobbish explanation that he had hoped a mixture of his own elite ancestry with her more down-to-earth heritage would produce robust offspring.

In any case, he showed symptoms of being in love. Encouraged by Emily, who still admired Sue, Austin poured out a torrent of emotion that led to his engagement. By that time, he already felt some doubts because Sue responded with a coolness and calculation he had not anticipated. Nevertheless, she was handsome and she easily ingratiated herself with Austin's parents. So the marriage plans proceeded. Only Vinnie disapproved, though she tried loyally to like Austin's future wife.

The wedding was celebrated on July 1, 1856, at the home of Sue's aunt in Geneva, New York. It is worth noting that none of Austin's family attended the ceremony, probably owing to Emily's increasing avoidance of strangers. At any rate, the newlyweds were soon established in the fine house the Squire had built them adjoining the Homestead. Sue called her own elegant residence the Evergreens.

The two Dickinson houses, behind their dense hedge along Main Street, were connected by a garden path that, at least for the next several years, was used continuously. Besides the normal sort of back-and-forth visiting between relatives who lived so near each other, a special bond tied Emily to Sue. For if Sue had used Emily as a means of furthering her social ambitions, a quite similar but far more significant process worked in the opposite direction. Emily used Sue— to test her own bold early flights into the realm of poetry.

We do not know when Emily, momentously, decided that she could be a poet, or how she came to arrive at her decision. Most probably her first efforts were spontaneous effusions, like the valentine message she sent the editor of an Amherst College student publication when she was only eighteen. There had apparently been an informal contest, but hers was the sole entry printed. Mostly in prose, it started with a comic rush of words that were recognized by a very few readers as inspired nonsense verse: "Magnum bonum, 'harum scarum,' zounds et zounds, et war alarum, man reformam, life perfectum, mundum changum, all things flarum?"

Over the years, two or three instructors at the college and a handful of other acquaintances gave her reason to believe she had a gift for expressing herself, both in prose and verse. As early as 1853, when Austin sent her some kind of poetic snippet he had composed, Emily playfully warned him: "I've been in the habit *myself* of writing some few things, and it rather appears to me that you're getting away my patent so you'd better be careful, or I'll call the police!"

But one of Emily's early sources of encouragement died tragically; others married and departed from her narrow orbit. She was left, as she approached the age of thirty, with a great need for guidance by an understanding critic. In effect, she appointed Sue to be the jury on which she tried out her every experiment during the years when she was painstakingly striving, alone, to reach the summit of literary artistry.

It was not an ideal arrangement. Sue's personality could not fail to cause friction that hurt Emily deeply, because Sue, upon becoming Mrs. Austin Dickinson, assumed the role of Amherst's leading hostess, regally entertaining her chosen elect and spreading unpleasant tales about those who displeased her. Though she refrained from outright war with any member of her husband's family in the first years of her marriage she and the outspoken Vinnie barely disguised their enmity.

Once Vinnie was humorously relating a dream of hers, in which she had died and had been unable to pick out the coffin she would like to be buried in, among the many offered for her inspection. Sue, quick and positive on any subject, smiled with a glint of spite. "Oh, Vinnie," Sue said, "have the handsomer one—and go in style!"

But it was Austin who clearly bore the brunt of Sue's headstrong campaign for social leadership, and of her sarcastic tongue. His idea of an enjoyable Saturday afternoon was a ramble through the woods around Amherst, searching out unusual trees that could be transplanted, beautifying the village. Sue's was to fill the house with swarms of shrill-voiced tea drinkers. Yet his grumblings about her turning the Evergreens into a "zoo" merely gave outward evidence of his private unhappiness with his wife; it could be no secret to the sensitive Emily that the marriage was making her dear brother miserable.

How, then, could she have persisted in flitting behind the hemlock hedge from the Homestead to the Evergreens, carrying scraps of paper on which she had carefully written new verses? We must answer that Emily, for all her shrinking timidity, had an iron determination when it came to her poetry. She needed a perceptive audience—and only Sue was available to her.

If Vinnie had been able to assist Emily this way, no doubt Emily would have preferred relying on her. But if Vinnie had possessed the necessary insights, she would have been a different sort of person, very likely incapable of submerging herself the way she did during the late 1850s, doing whatever she could for her elder sister who more and more displayed a deep unwillingness—or inability—to cope with many aspects of ordinary daily life.

By 1859, when Emily was twenty-nine, she would urge a favorite cousin in Boston to visit Amherst, writing to her, "You are one of the ones from whom I do not run away!" And her meaning was clear, at least within her own family. During that year, while Vinnie had gone to Boston for several months to stay with her ailing Aunt Lavinia, one evening two callers arrived at the Homestead. Assuming them to be strangers, Emily, as she often did in such circumstances, ran upstairs.

But it turned out that the men were family acquaintances, whose raised eyebrows at Emily's odd scampering suddenly brought her gradual withdrawal from most human contacts into sharp focus. Austin was at the Homestead that evening, and later he lectured Emily about her rudeness. Because Vinnie was away, Emily wrote revealingly concerning the episode to an older woman who was a close friend, asking whether a written apology to the men ought to be sent.

"When Vinnie is here," Emily told Mrs. Holland, "I ask her; if she says I sin, I say, 'Father, I have sinned.' If she sanctions me, I am not afraid but Vinnie is gone now. . . ." Thus we see Emily already depending on Vinnie to an extraordinary degree while her cringing from other people grew from just extreme shyness into something much more exceptional.

In these years she still left the Homestead occasionally, even accompanying Vinnie on a visit to another cousin during the autumn of 1860, shortly before her own thirtieth birthday. Why Emily was willing to go as far as Middletown, Connecticut, when she no longer dared venture forth in Amherst to see a loaf of her own rye bread awarded a second-prize ribbon at the local agricultural fair, is another insoluble mystery.

Yet Middletown, perhaps only by coincidence, was where a man from their area became a successful banker. There are hints that he wanted to marry Vinnie, and decades later he still would be a shadowy presence in the background. Amid all the uncertainties concerning his possible courtship of Vinnie, only one fact is indisputable: she did not marry him. In 1860, when she was twenty-seven, we must assume that she had already decided she could not leave Emily alone.

By then Vinnie had taken to sparing Emily even the discomfort of being stared at and stuck with pins by the seamstress who came to make their clothing. Because the sisters were so nearly the same size, gowns intended for Emily could be tried on by Vinnie. And Vinnie did more than merely mail Emily's letters. As if Emily considered that the eyes of strangers glancing at her handwriting on the outside of her personal communications unbearably threatened her privacy, she asked Vinnie to write the necessary name and address of every recipient of one of her messages.

But why did Emily retreat further and further from the outer world? Why did she hide behind a door when even some of her childhood friends came to see her at the Homestead? Why were the girlish gowns she continued to wear as she approached and then passed the age of thirty always, winter and summer, made of the same delicate fabric, and always white?

We do not know. Despite decades of effort by uncounted experts in the unraveling of literary and biographical and psychological puzzles, nobody has yet come up with an unchallenged solution to the numerous perplexities of Emily Dickinson's life. One of these is the myth centering on her supposed hopeless love for the Reverend Wadsworth, which Sue's daughter would, for her own purposes, publicize. At least half a dozen other candidates, male and female, have also been proposed as the fundamental cause of Emily's bizarre behavior; in each instance the thwarting of her passion is alleged to have brought a lasting breakdown.

Sometimes the stories include a soap opera flourish involving Emily's father. Whoever Emily's loved one might be, a scene is visualized in which the Squire furiously forbids his daughter to continue the relationship, and she, distraught but obedient, renounces all future happiness—indeed, renounces practically everything except eating, sleeping, and, secretly, writing poetry. The most melodramatic version of this scene even has Emily telling her father that nevermore, in his presence, will she speak a single word.

We have already noted Emily's pity for her father. That and the profound awe he never ceased to inspire in her make any such violent clash quite unlikely. On one occasion, when the Squire complained of having the same chipped dinner plate set before him two evenings in a row, we know that Emily quietly arose from the table, removed the offending dish, and took it out to a shed where she dashed it to pieces to prevent its offending again. And, according to Vinnie, the young Emily once screamed at the top of her lungs because their father whipped a horse. Otherwise, rage was not the way Emily reacted.

Yet it is impossible to doubt that Emily knew the supreme joy of loving, besides the anguish of blighted love; her poetry proves it. Nevertheless, only one actual romance can be documented, and that did not start until she was in her late forties. So most of the theatrical theories about Emily cannot stand up against impartial scrutiny. Of necessity, we must fall back on a simplified interpretation.

We have noted that Emily, for a few years, adored Sue. Surviving letters show Emily writing to Sue as if to a lover, although other evidence indicates that the relationship was almost certainly no more than an extremely intense schoolgirl crush. It is undeniable that Emily poured such a flood of emotion into her every contact with people whom she admired that they felt exhausted, drained, unable to fulfill her expectations, after spending any length of time with her.

Is it possible, then, that Emily, with her extraordinary intensity of feeling, *imagined* a number of love affairs? That she intensely exaggerated encounters that were much less overwhelming to the object of her love? And is it possible, too, that she eventually withdrew from the world because she herself could not stand the continual diluting of her emotional power from her poetry?

Certainly, around the age of thirty, she had achieved an unshakable confidence in her own genius. From whatever experiences she may have actually had, she realized that an ordinary married life would not allow her the concentration on her work it required. Also, she could hardly avoid understanding the personal cost of her chosen course, even as a spinster, because she had firsthand knowledge, despite her limited acquaintanceship in Amherst, that "female scribblers" were bound to be treated condescendingly.

That she would not endure. Thus, perhaps only subconsciously, she made her life itself a metaphor and, by her withdrawal, she showed that a genius who was a woman could not live normally. Given the playful side of her nature, were those white dresses just her playful way of saying she was married to her poetry? Still, we must keep in mind that Emily's commitment to her writing was hardly suspected at this period, even by most of those closest to her.

But all her family as well as their immediate friends knew that Emily's letters often included stanzas of verse. Because of the Squire's eminence in Amherst, even though changing political currents had ended his wider political career, and also because Sue could be completely charming when any celebrity came to town, the Dickinson circle included two major figures in the world of publishing. Both knew Emily personally—both saw at least a sampling of what she was writing in the letters she sent them. Neither, however, was much impressed. What were the reasons for their blindness?

Dr. Josiah Holland, husband of one of Emily's dearest friends, had given up the medical profession in favor of writing, although good-humored preaching was his real strong point. Under the pen name of Timothy Titcomb, he produced a stream of books that made him famous for several decades, but beneath all his jovial sermonizing, his ideas were extremely conventional. "To be a witty woman is a very dangerous thing," he held, and he advised young females against any activity that would attract the attention of the world. "Remain where God places you," he urged.

Even more specifically, in a book he wrote in 1858, he poked fun at "silly" young women who "take a literary turn, and, not content with any number of epistles to female acquaintances, send contributions to the press, which the friendly and appreciative editor kindly and carefully returns, or as kindly and carefully loses, or fails to receive." With such a patronizing attitude, Dr. Holland was scarcely disposed to discover any literary merit in Emily's verses. While he and his wife thought that personally she was delightfully unworldly, her poetry struck them as far too quirky for anybody else to enjoy.

So if Emily hoped that Dr. Holland would help her find an audience—and it seems that she did—no such help was ever offered. In another few years he would become the editor of the influential *Scrib-ner's Monthly*, but, friendly as the Dickinsons and Hollands remained until his death, the doctor never lifted a finger to promote Emily's writing. During this period he combined his own writing with assisting the other man whose failure to perceive any special worth in what Emily sent him must have hurt her much more severely.

Samuel Bowles edited a newspaper published in the Massachusetts city of Springfield, about thirty miles south of Amherst. The *Springfield Republican*, under his energetic direction, had attained national renown as one of the liveliest journals of the era. Every evening Emily read aloud to Vinnie from the *Republican*, while Vinnie sat sewing and making funny comments about the reports of outlandish accidents or train wrecks that particularly entertained her.

Yet Bowles himself, an outgoing husband who acquired quite some reputation as a ladies' man, fascinated Emily more than anything in his newspaper did. In fact, he is one of those candidates advanced as the probable love of her life, and, unquestionably, she wrote him nearly three dozen of her most mysterious letters. They sound ardent, even if they are often worded with such inexplicable subtlety that they might almost be written in a private code.

For instance, one of her notes to him starts: "Dear Friend. Are you willing? I am so far from Land—To offer *you* the cup—it might some Sabbath come *my* turn—Of wine how solemn—full!" What Bowles himself made of this we cannot say. Practically all we do know regarding his feelings toward Emily is that once, in a letter to Austin, he cheerfully relayed his best regards to "the Queen Recluse."

That she felt some sort of infatuation is fairly clear. Even so, we must wonder whether timid Emily, with her overmastering passion for poetry, might not have, for a few years, considered Sam Bowles mainly as her avenue to fame. In her letters to him she included verses that eventually would be among her most often quoted works. And in 1861 Bowles did print her poem starting, "I taste a liquor never brewed," with its magic second stanza:

Inebriate of Air—am I—
And Debauchee of Dew—
Reeling—thro endless summer days—
From inns of Molten Blue—

But Sam Bowles, at heart, was almost as conventional in his literary tastes as his good friend Dr. Holland. Over the years he printed just five of Emily's poems, always anonymously, using them to fill a few inches of space between news items, and each time he changed some words or punctuation marks to simplify her meaning. Although Emily may have loved him as a man, she hated having what she wrote meddled with in any way, so she inevitably lost her faith in Mr. Bowles as a judge of poetry.

Thus it must have seemed providential to her that in April 1862 one of the most highly regarded literary figures of the day contributed an essay to the *Atlantic Monthly,* telling "new or obscure" writers not to give up hope. Although Thomas Wentworth Higginson echoed some of Dr. Holland's dismay over the inferior drivel often submitted for publication, his tone was far more sensitive, especially in his willingness to admit that young ladies might compose something worth reading. Also, his comments about the importance of using words imaginatively struck Emily as applying directly to her own work.

So she audaciously sought help from the eminent Mr. Higginson. Though she was aware that he might have some knowledge of her family because he, too, had an irreproachable Massachusetts ancestry, associated with the Cambridge area near Boston, she approached him "at a slant," as she herself would describe her cryptic style. She composed a letter in which she somewhat oddly, but unmistakably, inquired:

Mr. Higginson,
Are you too deeply occupied to say if my verse is alive?
Should you think it breathed—and had you the leisure to tell me, I should feel quick gratitude—

I enclose my name—asking you, if you please—Sir—to tell me what is true?

With this seemingly diffident request, Emily enclosed four of her poems upon which she staked her future. If the noted Mr. Higginson found them "alive," she would achieve fame in her own lifetime— and, without any question, outwardly fearful though she was, Emily craved public recognition. Otherwise, why would she have dared to ask Vinnie to send this letter?

"I'm Nobody!"

HIGGINSON replied within just a few days. Hardly surprisingly, since this prominent writer and critic was a sort of mirror reflecting the accepted literary tastes of his era, he, too, failed to recognize Emily Dickinson's genius.

Instead, he sought further information. How old was she? Who were her favorite authors? Most importantly, did she have more poems she could send him? By his questions, Higginson certainly showed that his interest was piqued, but, to an extremist like Emily, his reluctance to commit himself about the verses she had already sent him must have caused acute suffering. "Thank you for the surgery," she started her second letter to him. "It was not so painful as I supposed."

Then she answered his questions—in her own slantwise manner.

"You ask of my Companions," she noted. "Hills—Sir—and the Sundown—" As to her reading, she mentioned Keats and the two Brownings and the Bible, unaccountably omitting Shakespeare, on whom she depended most of all. Indeed, throughout the rest of her life she would continue teasing Higginson with partial or mystical revelations about herself, always enclosing a few more poems.

Although Higginson could not avoid judging her work as too baffling for general appeal, he valued its originality sufficiently to keep answering her letters. Also, Emily herself aroused his curiosity, and soon he invited her to attend one of his lectures in Boston, after which they could have a good talk. In response, she urged that he come to Amherst, for she never left her father's house and grounds.

However, the Civil War postponed his promised visit; Higginson served as the colonel of a regiment of black volunteers. In Amherst these years of national crisis brought an equivalent personal crisis to Emily Dickinson. Something happened—again, we are in the dark about the details—but as a result Emily ceased using the garden path behind the hedge, cutting off all face-to-face contact with her formerly cherished "Sister" Sue. Eventually the hostility between Emily and Vinnie at the Homestead and Sue at the Evergreens would even be described as "The War Between the Houses" by some of their neighbors.

The turbulence of Emily's emotions must have reached an exceptional pitch in this period and, like so many other artists, she sought relief by pouring her feelings into a frenzy of work. Experts in the assigning of dates for her output estimate that she wrote at least a poem a day in the first half of the 1860s—a fantastic production, including much of her finest verse. Such concentrated effort undermined her strength to the extent that her eyesight was severely affected.

Then she did go to Boston for seven long months, staying at a boardinghouse with two of her younger female cousins she had never stopped feeling at ease with, while she went through a series of treatments by an eye doctor. His strict prohibition against her doing any reading or writing during her exile from Amherst made her feel as if she were "in Siberia." When finally she was told that she could return home, she wrote explicitly, asking that only one member of her family meet her at the railroad depot.

It was Vinnie, just Vinnie, whom Emily wanted to escort her back to the safety of the Homestead. Though their mother intermittently was confined to her bed by what seems to have been a form of rheumatism, she was in fair health during 1864, and she could have driven to call for her elder daughter. The Squire, upright as ever at the age of sixty-one, surely could have ceremonially welcomed Emily. Regardless of her break with Sue, Emily and Austin remained close, so he, too, would willingly have taken her home. Yet only Vinnie was requested, only Vinnie somehow soothed Emily's tense nerves as nobody else did.

Of course, Vinnie went to the station; she always made Emily's happiness her main objective. That is not to say that Vinnie merely selflessly looked after her sister, for even if there had been no Emily, Vinnie possessed much more character than the soft, romantic girl Joseph Lyman had thought he was courting. The immensely capable Sue had quite soon recognized Vinnie as a worthy antagonist, who could instantly find anything at the Homestead—from a lost quotation to a last year's muffler. And Vinnie, in society, could convulse any dinner table, all by herself imitating the whole church choir. Besides, she confounded her enemies with her trick of wiggling the tip of her nose when she chose to express disdain.

Because Vinnie never gave up visiting neighbors who were having troubles, meanwhile keeping the Homestead a showplace with the help of the loyal Maggie who came to work for the Dickinsons in these years, she became one of Amherst's favorites, generously sharing the flowers she grew and cheerfully adopting stray cats, usually harboring about half a dozen. With the passage of time, her tendency to make biting comments when someone said something foolish grew more pronounced, but New England had a large supply of women who never married, and it expected spinsters to develop sharp tongues.

Actually, most of Vinnie's remarks were flavorful, if somewhat abrupt. "I am the family inflater," she once told a friend. Upon being pressed to explain herself, she did so crisply. "One by one the members of my household go down, and I must inflate them." Yet Vinnie shared Emily's gift with words only to a limited extent, as one small folder among the mass of Dickinson archives proves. It contains about two dozen scribblings, showing that Vinnie did try to compose some verses of her own, but nothing in this folder is a bit memorable. Of course, the real reason she is remembered is that she was Emily's sister.

At least in Amherst, Emily already was acquiring the status of a mythical creature during the 1860s. Understandably, a certain amount of gossip labeled her as "half-cracked," and yet eccentric spinsters were no rarity then. Practically every town had its peculiar old maid, often a member of a leading family—even the famous Mr. Emerson had a maiden aunt reputedly as brilliant as he was, who chose to go around in a garment she called her shroud, and sleep in a bed constructed like a coffin. So Amherst undoubtedly felt somewhat proud of its own white-garbed recluse behind the Homestead's hedge.

Only children were likely ever to see her. At the Evergreens Sue, after five years of marriage, had finally become a mother, giving birth to a frail little boy named for his grandfather but always called Ned. Then a girl, Martha, arrived, and she, like the aunt whose name she had been given, was known as Mattie. Eventually a sturdy, extraordinarily lovable boy christened Thomas Gilbert—Gib, to everybody—joined his older brother and sister. With Ned, Mattie, and then Gib living behind the same hedge as the Homestead, Emily's solitary walks in Vinnie's garden were often interrupted.

But Emily adored the children and their friends. So much a child at heart herself, she joined their games, she baked them cookies, she made them funny little presents. If one of them forgot a jacket that had been dropped onto the grass in the heat of play, she would send it back via the Homestead's obliging maid, Maggie, its pockets stuffed with gingerbread.

Still, Emily never stopped writing. Whether or not the world paid heed, she could not live without writing poetry. "I'm Nobody!" she even exulted in one of her verses destined to be most often reprinted. Indeed, its second stanza has frequently been offered as evidence that she preferred anonymity because:

> How dreary—to be—Somebody!
> How public—like a Frog—
> To tell one's name—the livelong June—
> To an admiring Bog!

Undoubtedly, Emily shuddered at the mere thought of what public acclaim might do to her personally. Even if her era lacked the celebrity consciousness fostered by such inventions of the twentieth century as television, the kind of lectures that men like Mr. Emerson and Mr. Higginson regularly delivered in cities all around the country were not too different from the higher type of television talk shows. To picture the retiring Emily facing an audience of poetry fanciers in some Boston auditorium—not to mention New York or Cincinnati or Chicago—is just about impossible. Nevertheless, there are grounds for wondering whether her insistence, poetically and in some of her letters, that she would much rather remain a nobody might have been a case of sour grapes. Since the world refused to accept her on her own terms, she could do without the world!

Still, the audacity of her aims as she kept writing about matters like immortality indicated that she really was not so humble. Had her confidence in her genius been less justified, her attitude might even be described as arrogant. Despite her disarming way of pretending to possess a childlike simplicity, her self-assurance about her ability to deal with the broadest concerns of humankind came through clearly when she informed Mr. Higginson: "My Business is Circumference."

At last, in August 1870, Higginson's active schedule permitted a visit to Amherst, and fortunately he found the leisure right after he finally met the woman who had been sending him such extraordinary letters, accompanied by such queer and yet eloquent verse, to write a long letter home to his wife. As a result, we have the only reliable firsthand picture of Emily Dickinson at the peak of her poetic power, approaching the age of forty. After he briefly described the large country lawyer's house to which he had been directed, with its "great trees & a garden," he told Mrs. Higginson that he had been admitted to a parlor "dark & cool & stiffish, a few books & engravings & an open piano." Then:

> A step like a pattering child's in entry & in glided a little plain woman with two smooth bands of reddish hair & a face with no good feature—in a very plain & exquisitely clean white pique & a blue net worsted shawl. She came to me with two day lilies which she put in a sort of childlike way into my hand & said "these are my introduction" in a soft frightened breathless childlike voice—& added under her breath Forgive me if I am frightened; I never see strangers & hardly know what to say—but she talked soon & thenceforward continuously—& deferentially—sometimes stopping to ask me to talk instead of her—but readily recommencing. Manner thoroughly ingenuous & simple . . .

Emily spoke of her parents, slighting her mother as neither a thinker nor someone a daughter could take her troubles to; about her father she remarked merely that he read "lonely & rigorous books, only on Sunday." In general, she gave it as her opinion that women talked so much she dreaded them. She herself found Shakespeare such a source of joy that she wondered "why is any other book needed." Concerning her way of judging whether poetry had real worth: "If it makes my whole body so cold no fire can ever warm it I know *that* is poetry. If I feel physically as if the top of my head were taken off, I know *that* is poetry. These are the only way I know it. Is there any other way?"

But Higginson's main conclusion after meeting Emily was that he had never before encountered any person who drained his own nervous energy the way she did by her intensity as she conversed with him. "I am glad not to live near her," he told his wife. Mrs. Higginson's own summation of his report came a bit later. "Oh why do the insane so cling to you?" she asked him.

What Emily thought of Higginson we cannot say, but she continued to write to him, using an old-fashioned term for the office of teacher as her salutation. "Dear Preceptor," she would start letter after letter. Had she been more aware of his limitations, it is possible that she would have relied less on the conventional Higginson than on a girlhood acquaintance, the daughter of an Amherst College professor, and one of the few people who not only saw Emily's greatness but also repeatedly offered to help her gain the audience she deserved.

Helen Hunt Jackson, no longer a resident of Amherst, had herself acquired quite some renown as a poet and novelist. Though most of her own work would be forgotten after only a few decades, the fact that she—almost alone among her contemporaries—perceived the importance of Emily Dickinson's writing has given her a lasting, if secondary, place in American literary history. By an odd coincidence it was Higginson who aroused Mrs. Jackson's interest in Emily, and this may have been his major contribution to Emily's career.

Helen was so impressed with the verses he showed her that she immediately sent Emily the first of a series of increasingly urgent letters, all stressing the same theme: "You are a great poet—and it is a wrong to the day you live in, that you will not sing aloud. When you are what men call dead, you will be sorry you were so stingy."

Owing to Mrs. Jackson's insistent efforts, only one more Dickinson poem appeared in print—anonymously—but it is possible that Emily gained a new sense of purpose from this unexpected, enthusiastic endorsement of her work. Among all the mysteries clustering around her, none is as important, in the long run, as the one involving her own decision about what should be done with her poetry after her death. By 1870, when she passed her fortieth birthday, she must have realized that she and the world were too much at odds for her to achieve recognition during her lifetime. Then did Helen Hunt Jackson plant the seed that caused Emily to aim, instead, for the acclaim of future generations?

Nobody except Vinnie could have answered that question—and Vinnie never did. Even if she had, what she said might not be entirely trustworthy. For as Vinnie settled more deeply into old maidhood, her attitude toward Emily became so fiercely protective that she made some unbelievable statements because she thought Emily would want her to keep people from prying into what was none of their concern. Thus Vinnie vigorously denied knowing a thing about Emily's writing.

Yet it is utterly incredible that Vinnie could have been unaware of her sister's compulsive work. It took more than the flip of a switch then to provide heating and lighting. Somebody had to see that wood stoves were fed and that oil lamps were filled, besides ordering all manner of necessary supplies, including paper and ink. Even if Emily worked behind a closed door, it was Vinnie who bore the responsibility for making the work possible. Since Vinnie also addressed and mailed Emily's every letter, Vinnie knew exactly how often her sister was communicating with her many correspondents—or was writing something else.

Despite the spaciousness of the Homestead, it appears, too, that Emily and Vinnie still shared the same bedroom. On the few occasions when Vinnie went away to visit relatives or friends, Emily plaintively told Mrs. Holland or other confidantes about her own terror of the shadows, without her sister's guardian presence. So it is altogether inconceivable that Vinnie had no idea Emily was assembling hand-sewn little booklets filled with her penmanship and was stashing them away neatly in a large box.

We know that Emily looked down on Vinnie intellectually, so Emily might not have let Vinnie read her hoard of verses. Nevertheless, these sisters had, over the years, developed such a deep intimacy that they could communicate on many subjects without any need for words. And Vinnie, by now, depended on Emily as much as Emily depended on her because it was Emily who gave a meaning to her own life.

Possibly they never spoke a word about the future. But not only was Emily the elder; her fragility and her susceptibility to bouts of inexplicable illness made it a matter of unexpressed certainty that Vinnie would inevitably survive her. We are almost forced to assume, therefore, that, gradually, and perhaps spurred by Helen Hunt Jackson's praise of Emily's poetry, both sisters came to realize what Vinnie's greatest service to Emily would be. She would give the world Emily's poetry, after Emily's death.

Death was a subject Emily had always dwelt on with a particular intensity; it was never far from her thoughts. Yet neither she nor anyone else foresaw how soon and how severely her private universe was about to be shattered. Approaching her forty-fourth birthday, she endured her first devastating experience of a death in her own family.

Her father, at the age of seventy-one, gave no sign of weakening. Indeed, he had allowed himself to be persuaded to run again for public office, winning election to the Massachusetts legislature, where he hoped to lead a campaign in favor of greater state aid for the local railroad he had played a major part in founding. Aloof as he was personally, Edward Dickinson had effectively contributed to Amherst's every project for community betterment ever since his marriage nearly half a century earlier.

Besides serving as treasurer of Amherst College, he had helped to establish the town's newer Agricultural College, which would evolve into the main campus of the University of Massachusetts. The area's outstanding agricultural fair owed much to his organizing talents, as did other civic improvements as diverse as a hospital and the local telegraph office.

Although the personality of the Honorable Edward Dickinson remains an enigma, there is evidence that a warmer man, who wished he could be more outgoing, was hidden beneath his extreme austerity.

Once when he was striding home from his law office, he noticed an amazingly vivid display of northern lights in the sky overhead. Instantly he crossed the street to approach the church, and with his own hands he tugged at the bell rope to alert all his neighbors that something exceptional was happening outdoors.

Then, on his last afternoon in Amherst before going to Boston for the legislative session, he almost expressed affection for his elder daughter. Emily spent that entire afternoon sitting with him, just the two of them, after she had sent her mother and Vinnie off to do an errand. Though ordinarily she would have stayed upstairs by herself, she somehow felt no impulse for solitude.

Whether Emily and her father talked much during these hours she did not say later. Perhaps she read aloud to him from the *Springfield Republican*. But as the afternoon drew toward its close, her father remarked that he "would not like it to end," and Emily felt "almost embarrassed," because he so rarely voiced any sort of feeling. It relieved her that Austin arrived as the unusual words were still vibrating. To cover her confusion, she suggested that the two men go walk a bit in the garden.

The next morning Emily woke her father in time to catch his train for Boston—and then "saw him no more." In Boston, while he was delivering his planned address on a cruelly hot day, the Honorable Edward Dickinson felt faint and retired to his hotel where, shortly afterward, he died. It was June 16, 1874, a date that would mark a profound upheaval for every occupant of the Homestead.

Of Love and Death

EMILY stayed in her room during her father's funeral, prostrated by the sudden removal of the rocklike figure at the center of her private universe. Even Austin suffered a deep emotional crisis, and for the next several months he seemed utterly bewildered. Only Vinnie went through the burial ceremonies, then the rigors of the ensuing weeks, without breaking down.

It was Vinnie, representing her whole family, who somberly accepted the condolences of scores of neighbors desiring to pay their respects. Often she wept as they offered their sympathy, but she carried on despite her tears. Her sense of duty gave her strength, though gradually her sense of humor also aided her. In effect the new head of the household, because her mother proved almost helpless

170

under the stress of widowhood, Vinnie did whatever she thought needed doing—including swearing.

For she decided that every family must have someone able to say "Damn!" Thus she practiced pronouncing the expletive until, when she was forty-two, she became quite an expert imitator of her father in this department. If the butcher boy brought stew meat instead of the roast she had ordered, she might confound him triply: "Damn, damn, damn!"

Meanwhile Emily slowly resumed her accustomed habits of baking and writing, even though her mind dwelt more and more on the supreme mystery of death. As the months passed, she drew solace from creating a sacred image of her father, exalting him beyond human dimension. But all too soon a new calamity turned her attention toward her other parent.

On June 15, 1875—one day before the first anniversary of the Squire's fatal collapse—his widow could not rise from her bed. When Vinnie summoned a doctor, he spoke reassuringly to Mrs. Dickinson, but in the hallway after he had left her room, his face was solemn as he gave Vinnie his diagnosis. Her mother had had a stroke, he said. The resulting paralysis might last only briefly, or it might be permanent. While medical science could not cure her, perhaps diligent nursing would build up her strength and lead to at least a partial recovery.

Most particularly, the doctor told Vinnie, it was imperative that her mother be fed regularly. Beef tea, custard, any simple foods she might be willing to swallow should be made available every few hours. Emily, hiding behind a door, was listening intently. The instant the doctor departed, she hurried to the kitchen, bent on preparing a tempting little tray.

Thenceforth, tasty soups and puddings, presented on the prettiest of the Dickinson china, with miniature bouquets of flowers accompanying every meal, would be Emily's daily preoccupation. Vinnie, assisted by Maggie, remained in charge of the housekeeping and served as her sister's "Soldier and Angel"—who but Emily could have put it so aptly? Vinnie's determination to shield her from any frightening contact with the outer world was dauntless. One early summer evening, when the sky turned red because Amherst's worst fire was burning fiercely a few blocks away, Vinnie kept soothing the terrified Emily at the window of their bedroom. "It's only the Fourth of July," Vinnie valiantly lied.

Even so, it was Emily who bore most of the drudgery involved in caring for their invalid mother. Although Mrs. Dickinson eventually improved to the extent that she could spend several hours a day propped in an easy chair upstairs, never again would she walk unaided or take more than a few steps leaning on Emily or Vinnie. In adversity, she displayed a sweetness of character, however, that endeared her increasingly to both her daughters. But it was, alas, undeniable that this mother had turned into her children's child.

Over the next eight years the sisters did everything possible to preserve the frail old woman they came to love far more than they had loved her before her illness. But if each slight change in her condition absorbed them, they by no means lacked other concerns. Indeed, the outwardly sedate Homestead saw an amazing range of passionate emotion during those eight years.

In this period Emily had the only romantic adventure of her life that we can be sure really happened. Another cache of old letters, uncovered in the 1950s, provides positive evidence of Emily's attachment, besides indicating that she even considered marrying. It is an astonishing story.

Following her father's death, Emily had found a special comfort in talking about him with one of his old friends, Judge Otis Lord. The Judge had run for office on the same ticket as the Squire years earlier, and because they cherished similar political convictions, the tie had continued despite the distance between Amherst and the Massachusetts seacoast town of Salem, where the Lord family resided. After several decades, more than just politics bound the two families, so the Judge and his wife had naturally hastened to the Homestead as soon as word of the Squire's death reached them.

In the next few years Judge Lord's visits provided the brightest hours of Emily's uneventful existence. He appeared, on the surface, to be a pompous man, whose dignified bearing suited his judicial career, but he also had a playful wit, which began to captivate her. Yet not until his wife died—in 1877, three years after Emily had lost her father—did the relationship deepen.

Emily then was forty-seven. Judge Lord, only nine years younger than her father would have been, had reached the age of sixty-five. Still, with the fervor of youth, they both fell in love.

If that sounds startling, it is actually not too surprising that they were intensely drawn to each other. Emily had always felt such awe when death claimed any person of her acquaintance that she showered the bereaved with her unique words of sympathy. So she must have lavished pity on Judge Lord after his wife was taken from him, and in the highly charged atmosphere of mourning, the growth of a new closeness flourished. Something quite similar had happened with shy young Harriet Beecher and Calvin Stowe.

But how could Emily Dickinson possibly leave the Homestead to become the wife of a prominent public official in distant Salem? Though scraps of her letters to Otis Lord hint that she thought of marrying him, there were many obstacles preventing their union, and we know she remained in Amherst. Like so much else in her life, however, her love affair is surrounded by uncertainties. All we can be sure of, from the fragments of correspondence that unaccountably were saved, is that she openly adored the Judge and that her feeling was reciprocated.

Besides her shrinking timidity, no doubt Emily's commitment to nurse her mother blocked her marriage. Yet her continuing need to pour her energy into her poetry would have restrained her even if nothing else had. As she approached the age of fifty, her feverish output of verse did diminish somewhat, but many of her most complex poems were written during the years when she was imploring "my lovely Salem" to visit her.

There is one other factor that must have influenced Emily's decision against becoming Mrs. Lord. Her own exceptional dependence on

Vinnie had forged a chain that bound Vinnie as much as Emily, because by now, guarding Emily was Vinnie's main reason for living. Unfortunately, there are only faint clues about the strain that may have developed between the sisters when Emily fell in love. It is clear, nevertheless, that Vinnie endured a miserable six months.

Not long after the death of Judge Lord's wife, various letters mailed from the Homestead refer cryptically to Vinnie's going through a great "woe." Whether her unusual surrender to gloom had anything to do with Emily's sudden spurt of independence, making Vinnie feel useless, is a question that simply cannot be answered. Yet it is possible to guess that the two emotional states might have been connected.

It is also possible, though, that Vinnie herself had an unhappy romantic episode. We know that even a decade later the banker in Connecticut who had wanted to marry her was still on her mind, and perhaps some encounter with him caused Vinnie's untypical depression. That her woe stemmed from heartache rather than any physical ailment is the sole unmistakable conclusion we can draw on the basis of the limited information available. Since Vinnie fully shared Emily's intense preference for personal privacy, she herself destroyed any papers in her possession having to do with her own concerns.

This horror of gossip was not unusual in their day. Among families like the Dickinsons, the idea that strangers might have even the slightest knowledge of an attachment apart from marriage created a degree of alarm it is difficult to appreciate in our less conventional climate a century later. Thus we can scarcely comprehend the impact on Emily and Vinnie when their brother—in 1882—gave the Homestead an outright scandal.

The preceeding year of 1881 had started a sequence of severe shocks, which would increasingly undermine Emily's health. That March Judge Lord had been felled by a heart attack, and although he recuperated sufficiently to be deemed in no immediate danger, even visiting Amherst the following month, he was advised to retire from the bench. Since he was nearing his sixty-ninth birthday, Emily could hardly avoid contemplating how she could ever endure going on without him.

In these circumstances, the arrival within her narrow frame of reference of some attractive young neighbors provided welcome diversion. In August 1881 a graduate of Amherst College who had been hired to teach astronomy there, though he was still under thirty, took up residence not far from the Dickinsons with his charming, talented wife. At twenty-four, Mabel Loomis Todd was an accomplished pianist and painter, besides being the mother of an appealing little daughter. Mabel herself had grown up amid the best society of Washington, D. C., but she was fascinated by the simplicity and natural beauty of the Amherst scene.

As much as Emily shrank from making any new acquaintance, she soon felt such curiosity about this lively young neighbor that Vinnie sent a note urging Mrs. Todd to call at the Homestead. If the invitation showed Vinnie's attentiveness to Emily's least whim, it also demonstrated her willingness to challenge the imperious Sue at the Evergreens. For Sue had wasted no time in cultivating "Toddy" as her own latest social conquest.

Sue could still be enchanting when she wished, and Mabel had swiftly come under her spell. Unaware that Mrs. Austin Dickinson's antagonism toward her husband's sisters was common knowledge, Mabel blithely told her of Vinnie's note the day she received it. Just as blithely she added that she had already heard intriguing tales about the white-garbed Miss Emily, so she looked forward to meeting the mythical recluse and sharp-tongued Miss Vinnie, too. Mrs. Dickinson's reaction startled her new friend.

It was risky to enter the Homestead, she said ominously.

But why? Mabel's enthusiasm about every aspect of Amherst life made her press for more details. What harm could two spinsters conceivably do her?

Mrs. Dickinson replied in a tone of some satisfaction that associating with them was dangerous because neither of them had any idea of morality.

Oh! That entertained the cosmopolitan Mabel. Pray tell me the way they offend, she begged.

Sue Dickinson was not amused. "I went in there one day," she answered with her eyes glinting, "and in the drawing room I found Emily reclining in the arms of a man. What do you say to that?"

Mabel Todd merely murmured she had no explanation and let the subject drop. But her intention of accepting Vinnie's invitation was only strengthened by this odd conversation. It was indeed a most fitting prelude to the bizarre drama that would shortly embroil Mabel and all the Dickinsons.

During the next several months Mabel became a vivid presence at the Homestead, coaxing sprightly music from its parlor piano and enlivening winter afternoons with her deft sketching of woodland flowers. Although she never actually saw Emily, who remained hidden in back of the dining room door, they exchanged little gifts, via Vinnie, every time she came. To Vinnie no less than Emily, this high-spirited young woman was an exhilarating breath of fresh air.

Of course, the visits antagonized Sue. In countless small ways she had learned to irritate her husband's sisters—perhaps only because they would not accept her dictation humbly—but now she intensified her campaign of petty tyranny. Ever since the Squire's death, there had been problems over money; unmarried females were not supposed to handle more than trifling sums, so Sue managed to harass Vinnie increasingly by withholding payment of Homestead expenses.

But Sue soon had further cause for ire, even if Emily and Vinnie could not be blamed. Like them, Sue's older son, Ned, found Mabel Todd irresistible. He was twenty in 1882, a bookish young man who had never outgrown his boyhood sickliness, and his family had little hope of his surviving more than another few years. Much to the distress of both his parents, Ned fell victim to an overwhelming infatuation that made him Mrs. Todd's slave.

His attentions flattered her at first, then embarrassed her to the extent that she left town with her daughter and spent two months with relatives in Washington. When she returned, though, Ned broke his promise not to seek her company. Thus the stage was set for a nearly incredible New England spectacle. Its repercussions, Vinnie would claim, cut ten years from Emily's life.

For Ned's father undertook to prevent any resurgence of his son's passion, and in the process he himself lost his heart. At fifty-two, Austin had armored his sensitive nature beneath almost as stern an exterior as his own father, making the best of his wretched marriage by tirelessly serving his community. He, too, was treasurer of Amherst College and the pillar of every worthy cause for miles around. But Mabel Todd, then twenty-five, completely melted his defenses.

Walking together out in the countryside one warm September afternoon in 1882, they realized they were powerless to resist the feelings propelling them toward each other. As they both later confided to their diaries, they became lovers that afternoon, and the date would be the turning point of both their lives. Despite their marital commitments, despite the prevailing censure of adultery and the near impossibility of divorce, they could not give up the joy they had discovered.

Everybody close to them had to agree it was a mercy that, just two months after this relationship started, Austin's ailing old mother finally died peacefully. If she had had any suspicion about Emily's more guarded connection with Judge Lord, at least she was spared the blazing heat of the new liaison between her son and Mabel. For the Homestead itself had turned into their daily meeting place.

Emily and Vinnie, with their intense loyalty to Austin, unhesitatingly did all they could to help him. Since he had been in the habit of stopping to see them on his way home from his office late every afternoon, he continued the practice after the fateful September—only now Mabel joined him. Yet they both had such busy schedules that they were constantly having to exchange notes making or breaking other appointments. Vinnie, carrying their messages in her knitting bag, served as their private courier.

Even though the sisters were buoyed up by their belief that Austin was entitled, at last, to some personal happiness, all this excitement had its cost. The death of their mother had shaken Vinnie almost as much as Emily, and the feeling of being cast adrift that oppressed them made them especially susceptible to Sue's meanness. Inevitably she had found out what was happening, so her vengeful treatment of the sisters reached a new pitch of malice. "The Old Scratch," Vinnie grimly called her.

Mabel's husband took a completely different course. David Todd, a quiet and gentle scientist who worshiped his wife, behaved with such forbearance that it almost seemed he was encouraging the love affair. He admired Mr. Dickinson too sincerely to blame him, and he did not blame Mabel, either. Instead he simply accepted the situation, hoping that somehow time would solve everything. Still, he was not really as calm as he appeared, and in time he suffered a nervous breakdown which ended his teaching; he spent the last several decades of his life in a mental hospital.

So the furious antagonism of Sue perhaps saved her own sanity, though she certainly upset everybody around her. Austin's connection with Mabel Todd brought a virtually total break between the Evergreens and the Homestead. Only one unifying force gave some hope that eventually the breach might be healed.

Gib, the youngest of Austin and Sue's three children, was an exceptionally lovable boy. Handsome and glowing with health, he already showed unusual intelligence, too. Emily and Vinnie doted on him no less than his parents did, which made all Amherst—agog over each new rumor regarding the Dickinsons—guess that he might in some way dissolve the bitterness afflicting his family.

But in the autumn of 1883 Gib at the age of eight developed an inexplicable fever. Unbelievably, he sank into a coma. For the first time in fifteen years, Emily hurried along the garden path and entered the Evergreens to sit at his bedside. Her horror as his pulse weakened caused Vinnie to take her home. That night, while Emily went through a terrible siege of vomiting, her beloved nephew died.

Austin was dazed; even Sue broke down then. In a few days, when

Emily's alarming symptoms ceased threatening to kill her, too, Vinnie herself was treated by the family doctor for utter exhaustion. But instead of bringing a truce in "The War Between the Houses," Gib's death sadly solidified the enmity. It also left Emily pitifully weak. Too many deaths among her closest ties had sapped her strength— and more trauma was to come.

Only six months after young Gib's untimely end, in March 1884 Judge Lord succumbed to heart disease at the age of seventy-two. Somehow Emily remained on her feet for another two months, then early in May 1884, while she was helping faithful Maggie bake a loaf of cake, she saw a great blackness approaching her. When she regained consciousness, she was in her bed. It was the first manifestation of her final illness.

For two more years Vinnie waited on her sister day and night, handing her paper from time to time when Emily's craving to express herself temporarily reasserted itself. Vinnie refused to abandon hope until, at the beginning of May 1886, there could no longer be any doubt of the outcome. Then the ordeal lasted only two weeks longer.

According to their doctor, a kidney ailment was responsible for Emily's wasting away, and yet Vinnie would never cease believing that her darling sister had merely lost her will to live. Whoever was right, there came a morning when the fifty-five-year-old Emily scrawled a note to her cousins in Boston. "Called back," she wrote, and then she breathed her last—on May 15, 1886.

Four days later a cluster of mourners assembled beside a white casket in the Homestead hallway. By Emily's own direction, only a wreath of wild violets adorned it, and the funeral service was very simple. After the pastor of the local church spoke a short prayer, a visitor from Boston—Emily's "Dear Preceptor," Mr. Higginson—stepped forward. "I will read a poem our friend who has just now put on immortality used to read to her sister," he said.

It was "Last Lines" by the English Emily Brontë:

No coward soul is mine,
  No trembler in the world's
    storm-troubled sphere:
I see Heaven's glories shine,
  And faith shines equal,
    arming me from fear . . .

As his voice faded, Vinnie approached the casket and put two fresh lavender flowers into Emily's hand. "To take to Judge Lord," she gruffly told Mr. Higginson. Then six men who had worked at various times in the Dickinson stable lifted the white coffin and carried it through three fields filled with buttercups and daisies to the family cemetery.

Vinnie went home alone following the burial, but her awful sense of loss was eased by her knowledge that she had not finished serving Emily. She knew what she had to do now, and the next morning she embarked on the most important mission of her own life.

Vinnie Alone

FIRST, Vinnie emptied out drawers filled with all the letters Emily had ever received. She burned them, as Emily had requested, spending hours throwing one bundle after another onto a smoldering fire. Then Vinnie opened a large box whose contents she had not been instructed to destroy.

Trembling with excitement, she inspected the treasure her sister had entrusted to her. About sixty hand-sewn little booklets lay stacked in tidy piles, and Emily's distinctive script had traced patterns of varied dimensions across each page. It was poetry—nearly eighteen hundred poems altogether. Just seeing them gave Vinnie "a 'Joan of Arc' feeling," she later confessed.

Yet how could she bring Emily's genius to the world's attention?

Vinnie realized that the poetry must be published, but she had only the vaguest notions about the procedure for accomplishing this. So she began by swallowing her pride and carrying the box of the precious legacy Emily had assembled—to the Evergreens.

She knew that Sue understood poetry far more clearly than she did. Besides, Sue had the drive and the social connections that would enable her to gain a hearing from influential literary personages. Because she had written a handsome tribute to Emily that appeared in the Amherst newspaper, Vinnie assumed the enmity of the past had been forgotten.

What Vinnie had not bargained on, though, was Sue's unwillingness to exert herself except for her own purposes. She sent a few verses to editors she was acquainted with, but delayed and delayed doing anything about getting a book published. Meanwhile, she used some of the poems in her possession selfishly, reading them aloud at her tea parties so that her guests would say: "Isn't it *interesting* to go to Mrs. Austin Dickinson's tea parties!"

At last Vinnie lost her temper. She swooped down on the Evergreens again and seized the booklets she had lent Sue. They were *her* property, she cried, for dear Emily had left everything to *her*. Back at the Homestead, Vinnie scribbled a note that same day to the only literary figure she knew how to reach, imploring him to help her.

Mr. Higginson replied kindly but not very helpfully. He said his experience of having received dozens of Emily's verses in the mail made him feel she had been singularly gifted, but it had also made him aware that her handwriting was beyond the fathoming of busy editors who required manuscripts to be easy to read before they even considered whether or not to accept them for publication. So the material in Miss Vinnie's possession would have to be painstakingly copied if it was to be submitted anywhere, and he himself lacked the time to undertake such a project.

Vinnie had been teased too often about her own horrible ink blotches for her to imagine she could do the job Mr. Higginson described. Who could do it instead? Just one person came to Vinnie's mind, and despite the perils involved, she dashed off a note summoning Mabel Todd.

Mabel's love affair with Austin had by no means cooled, so Sue would be furious if she found out that her hated rival was assisting Vinnie. But a reluctance to antagonize Sue any further was merely part of the reason Mabel shook her head after she looked at the stacks of poems. She had done some writing for magazines, besides all her other activities, and she proceeded to give Vinnie a lesson in the facts of literary life.

Far more than just copying would be needed if Emily's verses were to see print, she patiently explained. For the pages of her little booklets were filled with crosses indicating words Emily had thought of changing, and alternate words were listed in the margins. It would be necessary to choose among all these variations, besides making other changes aimed at clarity. No editor would accept any manuscript for publication unless it seemed sufficiently appealing to have some commercial success, Mabel assured her pupil.

"But they are Emily's poems!" Vinnie exclaimed. Refusing to believe that they might be rejected, during the next several weeks she kept begging Mabel to start the needed work. Without Vinnie's perseverance, it is quite possible the world would never have heard of Emily Dickinson.

Even Emily's brother, who had seemed to be so proud of her, advised Mabel against heeding Vinnie's pleas. Did he try to read the little booklets himself? We do not know. But he warned the woman he loved that deciphering such a huge amount of his sister's writing could involve ten years of arduous labor. And who could say it would not turn out to be merely wasted effort?

Still, Vinnie would not stop grasping Mabel's arm until, almost grudgingly, the harried young Mrs. Todd agreed to give up four hours every morning. About a year after Emily's death Mabel finally began studying the material Emily had left. Then Vinnie sensed that the hardest part of her own crusade was finished.

For Mabel turned into the most enthusiastic of converts as soon as the peculiar handwriting she was reading no longer puzzled her. With mounting amazement she perceived that Emily truly had been the genius her sister proclaimed her. While Mabel copied verse after verse, she found herself uplifted as if by magic. "The poems seemed to open the door into a wider universe," she would later marvel.

Giving up her evenings as well as her mornings, Mabel spent more than two years completing the first phase of her promised commitment. By then she had done her best with about two hundred of Emily's least confusing poems, recopying them so they were fit to be inspected. Still, she felt a need to consult someone who could provide guidance concerning numerous words or punctuation marks. With Vinnie's approval she therefore went to Boston, where she showed her manuscript to the eminent Thomas Wentworth Higginson. After he read it, Emily's longtime "Preceptor" ruefully admitted that he had somehow failed to realize what a great poet she had been.

So it happened that a slender silver and white book—*Poems* by Emily Dickinson—at last was published in November 1890. Four and a half years had elapsed since her death, but Vinnie's elation as she beheld the beautiful little volume Mabel delivered from Boston erased everything else. For the time being, she was totally happy. And the book's reception did not disappoint her.

Not that the comments of reviewers were entirely favorable. Emily's disdain for the accepted laws of poetic expression upset many critics, and yet, despite their alarm, most of them could not avoid praising more than they denounced. As one instance, the Boston *Sunday Herald's* expert wrote:

> Madder rhymes one has seldom seen—scornful disregard of poetic technique could hardly go further—and yet there is about the book a fascination, a power, a vision that enthralls you, and draws you back to it again and again. Not to have published it would have been a serious loss to the

world. . . . I have read this book twice through already. I foresee that I shall read it scores of times more. It enthralls me and will not let me go.

Of course Vinnie was gratified by the praise, but she had expected no less. And she merely sniffed at the negative comments, considering them beneath notice. To her it was undeniable that Emily ranked with Shakespeare—and if the reaction of most readers did not quite match her own, she felt sure they would soon share her opinion.

Indeed, the book sold well enough to pleasantly surprise its publisher. Since poetry rarely made a profit, just five hundred copies of *Poems* by the unknown Miss Dickinson had originally been printed, but eleven times during the next two years new printings were ordered to meet the continuing demand. Furthermore, a second and then a third similar volume containing additional selections of Emily's work were prepared for publication by Mrs. Todd and Mr. Higginson.

As the "Joan of Arc" who had inspired all this, Vinnie herself became something of a celebrity. Instead of going about her daily routine at the Homestead with only Maggie and her cats to keep her company, she was likely to be interrupted by strangers while she stood outside hosing her flowers. Her gardening costume was most eccentric, consisting of a man's gray woolen shirt and a skirt of brown denim scissored indecently short—a full six inches above her ankles. Even so, Vinnie sometimes welcomed the unbidden callers; other times she shooed them away. It depended partly on her mood, but more on their attitude toward Emily.

If the visitors asked vulgar questions about her sister's friendships, or if she simply wished to be alone, Vinnie would not suffer in silence. When one of her neighbors complained that she herself was bothered by people who just dropped in, Vinnie spoke up tartly.

"Anna," she said, "you are a coward. When you don't want company, tell 'em so. Why, only last evening my nephew drove in here and said he had come to stay awhile. 'No, you haven't,' I told him.

'You weren't invited, so you turn straight around and go home again.' He went, but he didn't like it a bit. You are a coward, Anna, if you let guests bother you."

Yet Vinnie could be wonderfully hospitable, too. If her visitor seemed to have come because of a sincere admiration for Emily's work, the teakettle would be set to boiling. Then Vinnie would sit for hours reminiscing about her adored sister, even reading aloud some of her verses. She never tired of talking about Emily, and her own words attained a special eloquence as she did so. Once she wrote a letter in which she summed up Emily's gift with one short sentence: "Her power of language was unlike any one who ever lived."

That judgment was hardly unbiased, but enough people shared it to color the last decade of Vinnie's life vividly. Not only did she bask in the acclaim she had secured for her sister; she also benefited financially. Though the payments she received from the Boston publishing house of Roberts Brothers would seem small by today's standards, her share of the profits Emily's poems reaped was the first money Vinnie had ever handled herself. Until she was nearing the age of sixty, her every expense had been paid by her father or, after his death, by Austin.

So she immensely relished her new independence. In a sense she had earned it, and she displayed as much anxiety about the sales figures for the books as if she herself had written them. At the approach of the Christmas season in 1894, she scrawled a tense note to the head of Roberts Brothers: "May I ask if you will have an ample supply of 'Emily Dickinson' poems & letters for the 'Xmas' demand?"

By this time there were five Emily books. For the public's fascination with "the reclusive poetess of Amherst" had reached such a pitch that two more small volumes comprised of portions from letters she had sent various friends and relatives had recently been issued. Vinnie herself had done much of the work involved in collecting their contents, dashing off personal appeals to dozens of Emily's correspondents, asking them to send her any of her sister's communications they had saved.

Lavinia Dickinson toward the end of her life.

Nevertheless, the practical task of readying the material for the printer had, once more, been done by Mabel Todd. In this case, Mr. Higginson did not participate; he was an old man now, and ailing. Also, his eminent name no longer was required to convince the publisher of the soundness of the venture. As a result of Mrs. Todd's continuing diligence, she had become a literary figure herself.

But right from the first silver-and-white volume of Emily's poems, the matter of giving credit to Mabel had caused trouble. For it had terrified Vinnie when she found that the title page would bear an inconspicuous line saying these verses had been edited by the author's friends T. W. Higginson and Mabel Loomis Todd. As Mabel herself later told her daughter:

> Vinnie did not want my name on the book because she didn't want Sue to know that I had anything to do with it. Sue would have annihilated her if she could. They hated each other black and blue. She was scared to death of Sue, though she talked awfully about her. If I could begin to tell you what she said about Sue it would take the whole day.

Despite Vinnie's protests, which Mabel had tried to shrug off, Mr. Higginson made sure that Mrs. Todd's name was not omitted. Then the appearance of the book itself had at least temporarily ended Vinnie's panic. Her common sense told her Sue must have known for months what was going on, because she had a tremendous spy system. The main thing, anyway, was that *Emily* would now have the fame she had been too shy to seek in her own lifetime.

Although Vinnie managed to repress her fear during the next several years, it still kept haunting her. Being a person who could easily freeze any other enemy, why did she feel such a terror of Sue? That is another unanswerable question. But it is clear that Vinnie's inner cringing had sad effects.

By the time the two volumes of letters were printed, her relationship with Mabel had reached a sorry state. All traces of gratitude had gone, leaving Vinnie increasingly angry as she watched Mabel develop into the world's leading authority on Emily Dickinson. Perhaps jealousy would have made Vinnie resent anybody who seemed to be usurping her own place, though she could scarcely have pictured herself doing the literary drudgery Mabel did so efficiently. Nor could Vinnie, even at the peak of her self-confidence, have imagined she might take over Mabel's campaign of promoting the books by giving high-toned lectures in Boston.

Yet jealousy alone could not account for Vinnie's behavior toward the middle of the 1890s. Greed, undoubtedly, was involved, too, for her letters to Roberts Brothers indicate that she could not bear seeing any of the proceeds of Emily's work diverted into other hands. But without the scheming of Vinnie's dreaded sister-in-law, it is doubtful that her character would have disintegrated the way it did.

Sue Dickinson had her own compelling reason for detesting Mabel Todd. Year after year Austin and Mabel almost openly defied the moral standards of Amherst, while Sue's fury consumed her. One photograph of her, dating from about this period, when she had reached the age of sixty-five, shows a stout, imposing woman with an awesome glower and compressed lips. It can scarcely be doubted that such a woman would take advantage of every possible opportunity to exert her power.

And the sudden death of her husband, in 1895, gave her a chance that she seized. There were others who heartbrokenly mourned Austin, most notably Mabel, who would never cease to idolize him. His wife, though, made use of his departure—to mete out her own devious punishment.

Sue's revenge required the connivance of Vinnie and, after decades of enmity, it was no easy matter to win her aid. But Sue cleverly inflamed her sister-in-law's jealousy regarding the books until Vinnie's better judgment deserted her. A year after Austin's death, Amherst was stunned to hear about a fantastic lawsuit: *Lavinia Dickinson v. Mabel Loomis Todd.*

Technically, the court case had to do with a piece of property adjoining the Todds' yard that Austin had asked Vinnie to deed over

to Mabel. Vinnie had actually signed a piece of paper legally trans-
ferring the strip of land her brother wanted the Todds to have. Somehow, though, Sue maneuvered to convince Vinnie she could get the
transfer declared null and void. Everybody in town understood that
Sue was behind the ridiculous proceeding, just as they all realized its
basic aim was to mortify Mabel.

Its immediate upshot was a courtroom scene unparalleled in local
history. On the witness stand, Vinnie lied absolutely brazenly. She
swore that she had not signed the document bearing her signature—
she had merely written her name. She knew nothing of business, she
insisted. No, she had been the victim of some kind of trick.

Liar or not, Vinnie was cherished by Amherst as one of its own,
so the jury decided in her favor. The decision marked a total break
between Mabel and the remaining Dickinsons. Far more importantly,
it also stopped the process of publishing reliable versions of Emily
Dickinson's poetry for another half century.

Only three years after the lawsuit, Vinnie herself was overcome by
Sue's malice. Absurdly, the subject of their final quarrel was fertilizer.
When Vinnie learned that Sue had ordered her handyman to spread
the Homestead's pile of manure on *her* roses, Vinnie took to her bed.
Nothing Maggie or her friends could say consoled her, and she began
failing unmistakably. On the last day of August 1899, at the age of
sixty-six, Vinnie died.

If her life had worked out differently—if she had married and
achieved a personal happiness her warm nature had seemingly intended
her for, instead of diverting all her energy into serving her sister—
perhaps Vinnie would not have fallen apart as she did. Yet there can
be no question that, by her service to Emily, she earned the world's
gratitude.

Even so, she was soon forgotten. The day after her death, an Amherst College professor wrote a long article for the local newspaper
praising her "unique personality." But someone else, a quarter of a
century later, offered a briefer—and more acute—summary: "If Emily
had been less Emily, Lavinia might have been more Lavinia."

It was Austin and Sue's daughter, the only remaining descendant of Squire Dickinson. Brought up by her mother to consider herself above the ordinary run of Amherst residents, Martha had married an aristocratic if penniless European adventurer. Then she grandly adopted the title of Madame Bianchi.

And she made a career of doling out memories of her famous aunt, along with excerpts from the mass of poetry that had eventually come into her possession. Some of Madame Bianchi's contributions, such as her comments about Vinnie, were valuable. Still she must bear the major responsibility for spreading various romantic myths regarding Emily while she also prevented other, more qualified people from attempting to compile authentic texts of every verse.

Not until after Martha Dickinson Bianchi died, and the original handwritten poems went to Harvard's library, did a monumental three-volume edition of the complete poems of Emily Dickinson finally appear. By 1955, when these books were published, the story of Mabel Todd's connection with the Dickinson family was being put on the record by her daughter, Millicent Todd Bingham. Other diaries and caches of letters were providing new factual material for careful studies of Emily's whole life.

But even today, after so much effort has been expended, there are no solutions to many of the mysteries concerning Emily and Vinnie. In the annals of sisterly love, their story has no equal—despite the gaps that remain. It is certainly too bad that, right after Emily died, Vinnie burned a vast quantity of correspondence that would have helped to answer numerous questions. Who knows, though, what other hoards of old letters written by or about either of these remarkable sisters may any day be discovered in some attic?

Notes and Bibliography

Years ago, in a Vermont book barn, a faded green volume caught my eye. It was *The American Woman's Home* by Catharine E. Beecher and Harriet Beecher Stowe, and I bought it. That started my special interest in sisters, which would eventually produce this book.

For I was fascinated to discover that the author of *Uncle Tom's Cabin* had had an elder sister who wrote, too. What had *her* life been like? My curiosity about Catharine gave me a sort of hobby—looking into the sisterly emotional ties among outstanding women. Still, it did not occur to me to combine a few of my case histories and make a book of them. That was suggested by a very perceptive editor, Deborah Brodie, to whom I am most grateful.

But where did I find the information on which I could base factual—not fictionalized—life stories? During more than two decades of writing biographies, I have often been asked the question. Since I consulted such a multitude of sources in preparing this manuscript, it is not easy to answer. Because each pair of sisters in the preceding pages presented different problems, from the

192

standpoint of research, I think it may be helpful if I provide three separate short summaries of the material I used, including listings of some books that may help readers wanting to know more about the Beechers, the Cushmans, or the Dickinsons.

CATHARINE BEECHER AND HARRIET BEECHER STOWE

Hundreds of letters written by members of the amazing Beecher family have been preserved, mainly at the Stowe-Day Foundation's headquarters in Hartford and at the Arthur and Elizabeth Schlesinger Library on the History of Women in America on the Radcliffe campus of Harvard University in Cambridge. I owe warm thanks to the staffs at both for their assistance during my visits.

Of the dozens of books by and about Catharine and Harriet that I searched for firsthand recollections or factual background material, the following were the most valuable:

The Autobiography of Lyman Beecher, a treasure of Beecher lore filling two volumes, edited by Barbara M. Cross and published by the Belknap Press of Harvard University Press in 1961.

The Beechers: An American Family in the Nineteenth Century, the whole Beecher saga told by Milton Rugoff and published by Harper & Row in 1981.

Catharine Beecher: A Study in American Domesticity, a scholarly biography by Kathryn Kish Sklar published by the Yale University Press in 1973.

Crusader in Crinoline: The Life of Harriet Beecher Stowe, the best available biography of Harriet, written by Forrest Wilson and published by J. B. Lippincott of Philadelphia in 1941.

The Life of Harriet Beecher Stowe Compiled from Her Letters and Journals, a basic source book assembled by her son Charles E. Stowe, published in 1890 by Houghton, Mifflin and Company of Boston.

Saints, Sinners and Beechers, a lively compendium of family anecdotes by Harriet's grandson Lyman Beecher Stowe, published in 1934 by the Bobbs-Merrill Company of Indianapolis.

CHARLOTTE CUSHMAN AND SUSAN CUSHMAN MUSPRATT

Unfortunately, the Library of Congress in Washington has found it necessary to restrict access to its collection of Cushman letters and scrapbooks to microfilmed copies which are difficult to read. At Radcliffe's Schlesinger Library, however, I had an easier time because of an odd coincidence. Harriet Beecher Stowe's grandson Lyman Beecher Stowe had spent several years about 1940 assembling material for a biography he planned to write of Charlotte Cushman, until ill health prevented his carrying out his plan; but his typed copies of Cushman papers became part of his mass of Beecher papers that went to Radcliffe after his death.

Supplementing this basic source material, I relied mainly on two books:

Bright Particular Star: The Life & Times of Charlotte Cushman, an excellent scholarly biography by Joseph Leach, published by the Yale University Press in 1970.

Charlotte Cushman: Her Letters and Memories of Her Life, compiled by her longtime friend Emma Stebbins and published by Houghton, Osgood and Company of Boston in 1878.

EMILY DICKINSON AND LAVINIA DICKINSON

Because of its intense emotional complications, no family can be more fascinating—and frustrating—to write about than the Dickinsons. Emily's poetry, along with family letters that ended up in the hands of her niece, Martha Dickinson Bianchi, are now at Harvard's Houghton Library, while Mabel Loomis Todd's papers and Joseph Lyman's letters are at Yale; a miscellany of related material is at the Jones Library in Amherst. Although I looked into all these collections, almost everything of any significance has already been published in one or another of the specialized books Emily's life and work have inspired.

Among this outpouring, those I found most helpful were:

Ancestors' Brocades: The Literary Debut of Emily Dickinson, a careful account of Mabel Todd's connection with the poems and with Vinnie, written by her daughter Millicent Todd Bingham and published by Harper & Brothers in 1945.

The Complete Poems of Emily Dickinson, now accepted as the standard one-volume edition of Emily's poetry, edited by Thomas H. Johnson and published by Little, Brown and Company of Boston in 1960.

Emily Dickinson: A Revelation, also by Millicent Todd Bingham, and published by Harper in 1954, documenting Emily's love affair with Judge Lord.

Emily Dickinson Face to Face is the romanticized account of Emily written by her niece Martha D. Bianchi and published by Houghton, Mifflin in 1932. It elaborates on the same author's *The Life and Letters of Emily Dickinson* issued by the same publisher in 1924.

Emily Dickinson's Home: Letters of Emily Dickinson and Her Family by Millicent Todd Bingham, published by Harper in 1955.

The Life of Emily Dickinson, a masterly two-volume biography based on the best available evidence, written by Professor Richard B. Sewall of Yale and published by Farrar, Straus and Giroux in 1974.

The Lyman Letters: New Light on Emily Dickinson and Her Family also by Professor Sewall, putting Joseph Lyman's connection with the Dickinsons on the record, published by the University of Massachusetts Press in Amherst in 1965.

The Years and Hours of Emily Dickinson, a two-volume compendium by Jay Leyda of all the known major and minor events affecting or involving the Dickinson family, published by the Yale University Press in 1960.

Finally but fervently, I must thank the staff at the Vassar College Library not far from my home whose fine collection of books I was privileged to use in preparing this manuscript. Also, I am much indebted to Mary Lou Alm of the Pine Plains Library for securing numerous hard-to-find volumes for me through the machinery of New York State's interlibrary loan system. And I cannot forget the special assistance I received during the course of this project from Willa Beall, Franceska Blake, Roberta Bradford, Polly and Mike deSherbinin, Minky Johnson, Claire Smith—and my husband.

Grateful acknowledgment is made to the following for permission to reprint copyrighted material :

Amherst College Library : Portrait of Emily Dickinson on page 128.

The Folger Shakespeare Library : Photograph of Charlotte and Susan Cushman as Romeo and Juliet, 1846, on page 98. Photograph of Charlotte Cushman as Lady Macbeth, 1855, on page 81. Photograph of Susan Cushman on page 88. Courtesy, the Art Collection of the Folger Shakespeare Library.

Houghton Library, Harvard University : Selections from The Dickinson Papers.

The Jones Library : Photograph of Lavinia Dickinson on page 187.

Radcliffe College, The Arthur and Elizabeth Schlesinger Library on the History of Women in America : Selections from letters in Lyman Beecher Stowe's collection of Charlotte Cushman papers, Beecher-Stowe Collection, Schlesinger Library, Radcliffe College.

Stowe-Day Foundation, Hartford, CT : Selections from *Saints, Sinners and Beechers* by Lyman Beecher Stowe. Photograph of Harriet Beecher Stowe on page 43, photograph of Catharine Beecher on page 42, photograph of the Beecher family on page 50, and selections from materials from the collection of the Stowe-Day Foundation.

University of Massachusetts Press : Selections from *The Lyman Letters: New Light on Emily Dickinson and Her Family* by Richard B. Sewall, copyright © 1965 by The Massachusetts Review.

Yale University Library : Photograph of Lavinia Dickinson on page 129. Photograph of the Dickinson Homestead on page 148. Todd-Bingham Picture Collection. Selections from the Mabel Loomis Todd Papers and the Millicent Todd Bingham Papers.

196

INDEX

Cushman, Edwin (nicknamed Bub, later Ned), 87, 95, 105, 107–110, 114, 116, 117, 119
Cushman, Elkanah, 67, 70, 83
Cushman, Isabella, 83–85
Cushman, Mary Eliza, 68–72, 75, 79, 85–87, 90, 95, 96, 99, 100, 111, 117
Cushman, Susan. *See* Susan Cushman Muspratt.
Cushman, Thomas, 67

Dartmouth College, 50
Dickens, Charles, 101, 120
Dickinson, Austin, 123, 125–127, 131, 136, 137, 139, 141, 149–152, 162, 169, 170, 177, 178, 183, 189
Dickinson, Edward, 123–125, 136–141, 147, 154–156, 162, 165, 169, 176, 177
Dickinson, Emily, 122–191; born, 123; goes to Mount Holyoke, 127; returns to Amherst, 142; meets Charles Wadsworth in Philadelphia, 142; begins to write poetry, 151; becomes recluse, 154, 162, 163, 167; writes to Thomas Wentworth Higginson, 158–159; is visited by Higginson, 164–166; cares for invalid mother, 171–172; in love with Judge Lord, 172–173; collapses and dies, 179; first book of poems appears, 184
Dickinson, Emily Norcross, 130, 171–172, 177
Dickinson, Lavinia, 122–191; born, 123; to Ipswich Academy, 130–131; meets Joseph Lyman, 126; unof-

ficially engaged, 133; to Washington, 142; engagement ends, 145; visits Boston, 152; meets Mabel Todd, 175; urges Mabel to edit Emily's poems, 183; sues Mabel, 189; dies, 190
Dickinson, Ned, 163, 176, 177
Dickinson, Sue Gilbert, 141–142, 149–152, 155, 156, 162, 163, 175–176, 178, 182, 183, 188–190
Dickinson, Thomas Gilbert (Gib), 163, 178, 179
Dred, 49
Dutton, Mary, 19, 21, 26, 39

Emerson, Ralph Waldo, 72, 163, 164

Fisher, Alexander Metcalf, 9–10, 12–15, 28, 47, 50, 61

Gallaudet, Thomas, 20
Gilbert, Martha, 149, 150

Harper & Brothers, 33
Hartford Female Seminary, 14, 19–21, 58
Harvard Law School, 141, 149
Harvard Medical School, 53
Harvard University, 124, 135, 191
Hays, Matilda, 104, 105, 107, 109, 111, 113, 114
Hitchcock, Jennie, 130, 131, 133
Hooker, Isabella Beecher, 57–59
Hooker, John, 57, 58
Higginson, Thomas Wentworth, 158–161, 164–166, 179, 180, 182, 184, 185, 188
Holland, Josiah, 156

Holland, Mrs. Josiah, 153, 167
Hosmer, Harriet, 112
Hubbard, Mary Foote, 5, 6, 39

Jackson, Helen Hunt, 166–168
Jewett, John P., 45

Lane Theological Seminary, 22, 24,
    25, 31, 36
Lincoln, Abraham, 52, 59
Lind, Jenny, 136, 138
Longfellow, Henry Wadsworth, 106
Lyman, Joseph Bardwell, 122–126,
    130–136, 139, 140, 141, 143–146,
    162
Lyon, Mary, 20, 62, 127, 130

Macready, William, 100
May, Georgiana, 18, 25, 27, 54
Mayflower, 67, 70, 106
Mercer, Sallie, 90, 92, 93, 105, 109,
    111, 112, 118, 120
Merriman (Susan Cushman's first
    husband), 85, 86, 96
Mount Holyoke College, 62, 127, 130
Mount Holyoke Female Seminary,
    127
Muspratt, Ida, 105, 106, 114
Muspratt, James Sheridan, 101, 105
Muspratt, Susan Cushman, 65–120;
    born, 68; marries, 86; moves to
    New York, 86; gives birth to son,
    86; makes stage debut, 87; plays
    Ophelia, 88; divorce, 96; arrives in
    London, 96; plays Juliet to sister's
    Romeo, 97; remarries, 101; gives
    son to sister for adoption, 107; dies,
    117

National Era, 41, 44

Perkins, Mary Beecher, 8, 14, 17, 34,
    44, 57

Roberts Brothers, 186, 189

Scott, Sir Walter, 15
Seward, William, 108
Springfield Republican, 157, 169
Stebbins, Emma, 92, 115, 116, 118,
    120
Stowe, Calvin Ellis, 29, 30, 34–36,
    41, 44, 45, 47, 49, 54, 55, 62, 63,
    173
Stowe, Charley, 31, 40, 56
Stowe, Eliza (Calvin Stowe's first
    wife), 25, 29
Stowe, Eliza (daughter of Harriet
    Beecher Stowe), 31, 56
Stowe, Fred, 31, 53–56
Stowe, Georgiana, 31, 56
Stowe, Harriet (daughter of Harriet
    Beecher Stowe), 31, 56
Stowe, Harriet Beecher, 2–63; born,
    4; loses mother, 7; to school in
    Hartford, 15; starts teaching, 15;
    to Boston, 16; returns to Catha-
    rine's school, 17; to Cincinnati,
    23; writes *A New Geography,* 24;
    wins first prize in writing con-
    test, 26; marries, 30; becomes
    mother, 31; writes *The Mayflower,*
    33; moves to Maine, 37; begins
    Uncle Tom's Cabin, 41; *Uncle
    Tom's* huge success, 45; to Lon-
    don, 47; writes *The Minister's Woo-
    ing,* 51; visits President Lincoln,